The Return of the Quiet Stranger in the Black Hat

Paul John Hausleben

Cover design by Paul John Hausleben
The depiction of the character of "The Quiet Stranger in the Black Hat" by Mr. Amine Abidi
Cover photograph and all photographs by Paul John Hausleben

Published by God Bless the Keg Publishing
Somewhere, U.S.A.

ISBN: 978-0-9906979-6-1

The Return of the Quiet Stranger in the Black Hat

Dedication

To all of us who hope that within the dark corners and shadows of our weary world there shines an eternal light of hope, love, and joy

Contents

Acknowledgements

As always, a heartfelt thank you to Mr. Harry M. Rogers Junior, my friends and my family. Thank you to Amine and Alejandra for the cover art and depiction of the quiet stranger. Thank you to the mysterious man I met in a gin joint in Paterson, New Jersey in and around 1980 or thereabouts. If you had not been so quiet and so mysterious and if you had not worn that black, wide-brimmed hat on your head, then this character would not exist.

"Sometimes, in this life, in order to purge the pain and preserve our souls, our tears need to fall like rain."

Paul John Hausleben

01 April 2017

The Return of the Quiet Stranger in the Black Hat

When Worlds Collide

A story about blurred reality

Murphy

A story for the honor of our beloved companions

When the Night Closes In

Crime and fantasy mixed. Introducing, the crime-fighting Attorney Charles "Chuck" McCracken

The Circle of Life

A short story about the true heroes in all of our lives and about the cruelty of Alzheimer's disease. The wretched disease can steal a person's mind, but it will never steal a person's soul

Preface from the Author

The quiet stranger in the black hat returns, and so does all the controversy, which follows this character around. What started as a random and obscure character, created for the short story titled *Eleven Sentences*, has turned out to be a major influence on my writing. The ink was barely dry on the *Tales of the Quiet Stranger in the Black Hat* release when I received an email from a reader asking me when I would write the follow-up. At that point, it was a one and done series because; I had not even thought that there would be a possibility of continuing the adventures of the mysterious character. Oh, well. Now, in looking back, this little wandering or two, or three, in the fantasy genre turns out to have been adventurous, fun, and a wonderful ride for this author.

The main question, which surrounds the quiet stranger, is, of course, "Who the hell is, the quiet stranger in the black hat?"

I must say the suppositional ideas that poured in from readers after we published *Eleven Sentences* and *Tales of the Quiet Stranger in the Black Hat,* proved to be wonderfully creative and downright ingenious. Every theory that you could ever imagine, from an angel, to a superhero, to figments of the imagination of each character who encounters him, and many others, came across my desk and screen.

While I may someday reveal what the main idea that I had in mind was, when I created the quiet stranger, right for now, I think that I will keep those ideas to myself. It adds an element of intrigue and fantasy for each reader to enjoy in their own way, guessing and surmising as to his actual identity and origin. I will say that this collection of stories has a number of strategic clues and hints as to his actual identity, buried deep inside the pages.

Regardless, the quiet stranger returns within the pages of this book and this collection introduces a number of new characters that join him in his adventures. Some are good characters, some are evil characters, and the level of involvement in everyday life that the quiet stranger brings to this go around of adventures is quite a bit different from his previous appearances.

This collection started as a simple short story idea, and it was a story, which did not include the quiet stranger at all within the storyline. This happens very often with my ideas, I happily type along for a period of time, become disillusioned on my original intent, pace the floor, sip a little liquid inspiration (those fine Scotches are expensive, but amazing) return to the keyboard and off we go in a different direction. Now convinced that I had reached a dead end on that initial idea, the entire book took on a new direction. Before I knew it, I listened to some of those emails and clamor for more adventures from the mysterious character and the quiet stranger appeared from within the shadows of my own mind. He tipped his hat at me, nodded as only he can do, and boldly jumped into the pages of this book. The collection went off rather quickly and easily from there. The book was in a completed draft format, from start to finish, in about five days, including one long Fourth of July holiday weekend marathon of writing.

The quiet stranger in the black hat is still a character that I feel this world actually requires. It remains my hope and wish that somewhere in this great mysterious world, he actually, in some type of manner, does exist. I hope that he waits silently in the shadows to intervene in people's lives when we need him the most. What a comforting thought.

Maybe, who knows? After all, he really is a figment of *my* imagination.

On the other hand, is he? When I closely examine my life, I have many things that I cannot explain.

I enjoyed putting together this fantasy compilation, and it is my hope that you enjoy reading this book, as much as I enjoyed the experience of writing it.

Thank you for reading it.

Paul John Hausleben

01 April 2017

Prologue

In late August 2011, in a courtroom where the air conditioning systems painfully labored to keep the temperature just barely under the stifling level, attorney and city prosecutor Charles "Chuck" McCracken shook hands with his new partner in the prosecutor's office, attorney and assistant prosecutor Gordon Tolland. The two attorneys shared a quiet celebration on the conviction that they achieved this afternoon.

"Good job, Gordy. Your old man is looking down from his lofty perch, and he is very proud of you today. I am very proud of you, too. Big win for us!"

Gordon told his partner, "Thanks, Chuck. I have to admit that it does feel good. Seeing these poor people receiving some type of justice and the evil in this world receiving what they deserve is something that I rather enjoyed. After working with my father for all of those years, I must say that you adjusted rather well to having his rookie, attorney son following his example and trying to fill his shoes. Shoes that I am afraid that I could never fill."

Chuck rubbed the top of his flattop haircut; he loosened his necktie, and said, "Well, we will see. Ya might be surprised at how far you are going there, Gordy. Don't sell yourself short. You are a good one. Just need a little time. I do think you have a bright future ahead of you. Anyhow, yup, it is nice to see these bums get what they deserved. Swindling suckers, bilking old people out of their life savings. Glad they had some dough and were too stupid to bury some assets, so we could get some money for the good people. Did you see the smirks on their faces after the sentencing? Bet they ain't smirking tomorrow morning, when some big, sweaty guy is chasing them around the shower in the prison."

Gordon could not help but to laugh at his partner's rather rude and crude ways. Chuck McCracken was one of a kind, a man who did not mince words, back down from anyone or anything, but he knew what his father told him many years ago that Mr. Charles "Chuck" McCracken was one of the most wonderful, honest, and trustworthy men on the face of the earth. Gordon's father trusted him with his life, and now his son did too.

"Well, I am sure that they now have some regrets, Chuck. That might be one of them," Gordon commented, while he filled his briefcase with mountains of papers, and he collected pens, pencils, and other assorted items from the courtroom table.

"Say, Gordy, it is hotter than seventeen Hells in here. I am going to suck down a cancer stick while you kiss babies and smile at the women. You look a lot better than I do. You can answer the stupid questions that the reporters are gonna be asking ya in a few minutes. My attention span and congenial behavior does not hold up very well, when I have to answer the same questions, asked ten different ways, ten different times. I hope another case rolls around soon. You will shortly find out that I get bored without a case to chase down. Let's go downtown tonight and celebrate. We should try that new French joint downtown. You up for a night on the town?"

"I would enjoy that. Thank you, Chuck."

"Good, very good. I will call Michelle and let Jimmy know to pull the car around for us and for her to get ready. Takes my wife forever to get ready. Ya gonna bring that new chickee poo ya been playing grab-ass with? What is her name? She has nice legs and a great ass too!"

"Jennifer is her name, and yes, I will call her. Don't let Michelle know that you are checking out other women's backsides!"

Chuck laughed, yelled, "She knows already! I am painfully honest and I tell her that I got to compare them all to hers and that hers is still the best!"

He waved at Gordon while he walked quickly out of the courtroom. He stopped and greeted a few people, and then he disappeared from Gordon's view. Gordon continued to laugh at his partner's ruff and gruff and often lewd humor and behavior. He was quite the character.

Outside, in the designated smoking area, along the side of the courthouse, Chuck loudly spoke to his wife on his cellphone, "Yeah, baby doll, it was a big win for us! You will see the headlines in the paper tomorrow. The press is all over it. The kid did well. I am sure that his old man is proud. Be ready on time, will ya? Jimmy will swing by and grab ya. We are gonna go to the new French joint. I can't say it like you do, but you know it. Nous sommes . . . something like that. My French sucks. Okay, yeah, ya right. My English sucks too. Yeah, he is bringin' the chickee poo with the great ass. Nah, yours is better, baby doll. The best in the world! See you in a few!"

Chuck laughed as he hung up his cellphone, he reached in his pocket, pulled out a pack of cigarettes, stuck a cigarette in his mouth and then with the cigarette dangling precariously from the corner of his mouth, he poked around in his pockets for a lighter.

Before he could find his cigarette lighter hidden deep within the maze of his pockets, Chuck heard the distinctive "click" in the air of a lighter being struck. He turned to his side, and he saw the flame ignite. Chuck realized that he was lost in the euphoria of winning the conviction, as well as his wife's gorgeous figure, and that he had not heard the footsteps of the man who was now holding the lighter out towards him, when he had approached.

Chuck leaned into the flame, sucked deeply and spoke out of the side of his mouth, while lighting the smoke.

"Thanks, pal. I appreciate that. Hot as seventeen Hells, huh? Air is better out here, even sucking on these cancer sticks than it is in there."

Chuck pointed towards the courthouse building, turned around to look closer at the man who had lit his cigarette, and he was startled at the appearance of him. Chuck's eyes went up and down, while studying the man who was standing next to him, as Chuck observed what had to be the largest man that he had ever seen. He was immense, and the huge man now stood looming over Chuck while staring intently at him. The man snapped the lighter closed and placed it inside the pocket of a black vest that he was wearing.

Chuck mumbled, "Damn. . .."

The old prosecutor's eyes scanned the stranger standing next to him and he quickly determined that this man was not an attorney, or newspaper reporter, or anyone that he had ever met or seen around the old city before. In fact, he was not too sure who or what he was. It seemed as if he had been, until now, lost in time and magically appeared on the balcony.

The man standing next to Charles "Chuck" McCracken was dressed all in black. His black vest covered a perfectly pressed black buttoned-up shirt, and his sharply creased black trousers had no ripples or wrinkles. There was nothing out of place on this man, not a wrinkle, not a hair on his head, nothing. He was impeccable, immaculate.

His features were dark; he wore on his face a finely trimmed beard, closely framing a perfectly chiseled face, with piercing black eyes that remained staring straight ahead, emotionless, expressionless. On his head, he wore a wide-brimmed black hat, pulled down to where his facial features were not easily seen, but still visible. On his feet were highly polished black boots, buffed to a mirror shine. If you bent down and looked at them, you could see your reflection in them.

"Nous Somme Du Soleil," the man in black said to Chuck while speaking in a deep, melodious voice. The French accent rolled off his tongue very elegantly.

Chuck recovered when he realized that the man must have overheard his conversation and his stumbling over the name of the restaurant. He also must have heard the comments about various female attributes.

"Oh yeah, thanks, big guy. Is that how you say it? Got it, I think. What the hell does that mean?"

The man tipped his hat, and in a deep, melodious voice, he told Chuck, "It means that we are of the sun, and we can see. That might be helpful down the road, Chuck. Helpful, when the night closes in. At least, there will always be light for us to see."

Before Chuck could answer, or even react, the man tipped his hat, smiled, turned around and briskly walked away.

Chuck recovered and called out, "Hey, thanks, big guy! Say, do I know you?"

The man did not turn around or answer. Chuck watched and listened as he noticed that his boots made a distinct clicking noise as they struck the sidewalk while he walked away.

Chuck watched and puffed gently on his cigarette while he pondered some thoughts aloud, "Sharply dressed, dude. His boots make a cool ass clicking noise. Must have metal tips on those boots. Wonder, why he snuck up on me and I didn't hear 'em with those clicks? Muss'be slippin' in my old age. Damn, that was friggin' weird. It was as if he just appeared outta nowhere. Big guy, in fact, the biggest damn person that I've ever seen. Kinda have a strange feeling that we will meet again someday. He did not just show up here to give me some bullshit French lesson and light my cancer stick. Nope, I can tell. Hope he is a good guy, would hate like hell to have to tangle with his big ass. He would squish me flatter than I am about to grind out this cigarette butt."

Chuck shook his head, pondered his thoughts for a moment, and then went with his gut reaction.

Charles "Chuck" McCracken always went with his instincts.

He spoke his thoughts aloud once more, "For some reason, I have a strange feeling that he is a good guy, in fact, a really, good guy."

The cagey, old attorney stood there for a time, finished the cigarette, and took a few last puffs. He listened and watched until the quiet stranger in the black hat disappeared from his view and he could no longer hear the click of the metal tips of his boots on the sidewalk. Then, after one last drag, Chuck tossed the spent cigarette on the ground, placed his foot over the smoldering cigarette butt and with a few hard twists, he twisted the end of the smoke underfoot until the light went out.

When Worlds Collide

Part 1

Where Reality Begins

Humphrey J. Whitehouse always thought that there was nothing on the face of the Earth prettier, or more quieting to a person's soul, than a field of undisturbed snow. He seldom had the opportunity to see one; however, the one time that he did, it carved out a profound niche of impact inside of his mind forever. His wonderful experience occurred when he was young, ten or eleven or thereabouts, and on a holiday with his parents, visiting some distant relatives in upstate New York.

The relatives owned a large piece of property and one morning, after snow had fallen all the previous day and evening, Humphrey escaped the confines of the house. He had received very rare permission from his overly protective mother to go outside and explore on his own, all alone.

His mother was always very protective of him; after all, he was a fragile young man, prone to be sickly, prone to be cautious; an only child. Humphrey was very timid, very intelligent and highly introverted.

His school teachers all noted on his reporting cards how, "Humphrey, did not play well with others."

His behavior frustrated his socially active father and invoked protectiveness in his mother. Humphrey was her only child; she was not going to allow anything at all to hurt him or upset him.

Finally, outside, alone, exploring, as all young boys should always have the freedom to do, Humphrey stood on the edge of the field of his relative's property. The day broke clear and cold, a winter wind gently skated across the field and moved some gentle wisps of tall grass that poked their seed heads above the deep snow. There, in the quiet of the morning, Humphrey felt more content than he ever had. He had never seen any sight more captivating, more beautiful and more enthralling, than staring out upon what seemed as if it were miles upon miles of undisturbed snow. The sunlight glistened inside a few sparkles of the piled snowflakes, and it felt as if they were speaking to Humphrey's heart and soul.

It was so perfect, so calm, and the vision never left him, ever. . ..

Forever more, to Humphrey J. Whitehouse, when he needed to retreat to a calm place, he always returned to the field of snow in his mind. There, he could not be disturbed. All of his life, he longed to return to the field of snow.

Humphrey J. Whitehouse, now some thirty or so years removed from the edge of that snow-covered field, should have been basking in his success. He was still introverted. In fact, the media labeled him as preferring seclusion, which was, actually, an accurate description. The same media also labeled him a, "Quiet genius."

You see; while his school teachers would habitually note his inability to play with others, what they praised was his incredible talent to draw and the amazing art concepts, which he could create. Specifically, Humphrey could draw cartoons and caricatures of such incredible skill, depth and spontaneity that they were truly astounding.

He would look very briefly at someone, take a piece of paper and routinely draw an instant cartoon or caricature of the person.

His talent was amazing. No formal training required. It was all very natural for him.

Often, when the schoolyard bullies would pick on and poke fun at the lanky, skinny, kid wearing thick eyeglasses standing slumped shouldered, alone in the corner of the schoolyard, Humphrey would pull out the ever-present pad and pencil, which he kept in his back pocket. Humphrey would retaliate in a non-confrontational manner by drawing a cartoon of the bully, and the drawing would emphasize the bully's outrageous behavior. Humphrey did not physically fight back, but his ability to draw an instant cartoon of a volatile situation was all that was required to deflate a situation. It garnered him instant admiration. Even from his greatest critics and detractors!

Now, as the cartoonist and creator behind the single, largest cartoon strip in syndication in the publishing world, Humphrey J. Whitehouse should have been at the top of the world, but he was not.

His efforts at producing the weekly strip known as *Where Reality Begins* brought in untold millions. It spawned a cult following and from the roots of a simple cartoon, evolved an empire of tee shirts, coffee mugs, books, pictures, posters, calendars with the "Best of Where Reality Begins" sample strips for each month, all the usual offerings of the by-products of success.

An idea for a cartoon strip, which Humphrey had while still in high school, had created a worldwide empire, yet, in looking at how Humphrey lived his life, you would never realize it. His autobiographical strip about an introverted man, who does not fit in with society, hit the mark with millions of readers and the critics happily called him, "The world's greatest cartoonist! A man with keen insight to hit a nerve consistently every time, within six individual frames of his strips."

Humphrey lived in New Jersey, in a small, one-bedroom condominium in a high-rise building, located not too far from one of the main outer bridge crossings over the Hudson River. It was not a meager address, but for a man of Humphrey's means and wealth, it could not, by any description, ever be considered, overly extravagant or affluent.

Comfortable was a more accurate description. That is exactly the way that Humphrey J. Whitehouse wanted it to be—comfortable.

He socialized with no one, shunned interviews, and never attended galas, shows or events where the media highlighted or promoted his work. He kept to himself, just as he had his entire life. He left all the socializing, hobnobbing, and promotional work to his agent. His lawyers and accountants handled the business end, and Humphrey chose to stay in his creative enclave and do what he did best and that was to create.

Humphrey J. Whitehouse was now around forty years of age, and he never married. In fact, he had only ever dated a handful of women; he was tall, and he still wore his trademark, thick eyeglasses, and while no one would consider him to be a movie star in his appearance, he was an attractive man. He kept a fine beard and moustache, trimmed to perfection, wore his hair a little long for this era in time, and he dressed casually, but never sloppily.

His parents both passed away a few years ago. He had a few distant relatives still alive, but other than an occasional card around the holiday time of the year, he had no actual contact with any of them.

He spoke to his agent, his publisher, an accountant or two and Humphrey went to an intense business meeting about twice a year at his lawyer's office, and other than that, life was always the same.

He churned out cartoon strip after strip, staying months and months ahead of his deadlines, often creating strips in a magnificent outpouring of creativity that would last all hours of the day and night. Drawing, creating, mixing his main character, who was a tall, odd, geeky man, (an actual mirror image of Humphrey) that he named "Egbert," in with a smattering of other oddball characters, who all interacted with Egbert and either contributed to his awkwardness, or somehow, managed to create confusion in his daily life. The master behind the creativity always managed to place Egbert into an awkward situation of daily life, a situation in which every reader could relate to within his or her own lives. Another fascinating aspect of the cartoon strip was that Egbert never ventured far from the office where he worked, or from his own home. Those two locations were the only places ever featured in the strip, and the cartoon strip, in many ways, paralleled the creator's own life. No vacations, no day trips, no celebrations of any sort. Readers from every corner of the world loved how the awkward Egbert always managed to persevere despite the humdrum life he led, and the odd situations he became embroiled in. It was, in fact, unadulterated genius. There was no doubt that his cartoon strip was captivating.

It was now the week after Thanksgiving, in and around the year 2014 or thereabouts, and Humphrey J. Whitehouse was at his usual writing post, while pondering his next cartoon strip. The Christmas season madness was already underway, and every year, Humphrey pulled poor Egbert into some type of Christmas calamity, only eventually to celebrate Christmas alone, in his home with a Christmas tree that did not light, or a meal burning up in the oven, or some kind of other malady to make a reader sorry for the poor soul. Another humdrum holiday. It seems as if it had become a tradition.

However, this year, something inside, and something deep down within Humphrey, told him that his approach needed to be different this year. It was time for a change. Why was it the time to change things around a bit, he could not actually say; but he just knew it was time. It was a different feeling, very different, and rather than some humorous, cantankerous situation to embroil poor Egbert in, Humphrey felt it was time to draw something serious, something heartfelt, something that he felt was missing in his life and place it into the strip.

He leaned back on the stool in front of his drawing table; he sighed, stuck his pencil in his ear, and folded his arms. He needed to quench this idea, think about it for a long, long time, not to be too hasty in such an abrupt turn of directions. After all, the fan base would be in shock! Humphrey jumped off the stool, paced the floor back and forth a few times. He stopped and stared out the window and then stepped out onto his deck. He was about fifteen stories in the air here, and the view into Manhattan across the river was inspirational. All those millions of lives over there in the city. What is really going on over there? Is that actually where reality begins?

Humphrey stared into the city for a long time, writer's block was not something he usually dealt with, and this feeling, while it was not actually a writer's block, was quite a different feeling.

It was actually a directional block!

He made a final decision, always siding with his gut feeling, which never steered him wrong in the past, and he had little doubt that this time would be any different. He walked back into the living room, slid the door closed behind him, and left the deck and the view behind him. Jumping back on the stool, he drew with a newly discovered fervor. He now became convinced that it was time to change it up, mix it up. He had grown stale, grown complacent, and he wanted to live his own dreams for reality within his own creation. Perhaps, live vicariously through his character's fictional lives. Let the cartoon strip take on a life of its own.

"Yes, let's begin right now," Humphrey spoke aloud to the four walls of the room, while he set up the scene for the strip to live his own dream.

It was a vivid dream within Humphrey's mind, a dream to once again stand on the edge of the field of snow. To see it again, glistening, undisturbed, untouched, and to feel again the exhilaration that he felt that one time so long ago within his own soul.

At first, Humphrey knew and felt in his heart that the reaction of his publisher, when he saw the strips he planned for the holiday season, would be one obstacle to deal with. He predicted that he would first shock his editor's mind, and upon recovering from the shock, then his editor would protest the new direction and try to talk Humphrey out of this idea. Ultimately, they would have to side with the creator, they would have no choice; there was too much at stake. Then the reaction of the majority of the readers of "Where Reality Begins," would squarely fall somewhere between shock, awe, and outrage.

Still, Humphrey had to draw this because he knew that he had to draw his dream for reality.

The first strip, which Humphrey drew, featured the perpetually geeky Egbert, boldly standing up to characters who he usually meekly cowered to and retreated from, whenever he stated his usual docile point of view. On the first frame of the strip, planned for right after Thanksgiving, Egbert boldly states that he is taking an extended vacation for the Christmas holidays.

He proclaims, how, "He is leaving his position for a long overdue vacation and he will not have his cellphone with him, nor will he have email or text capabilities. His co-workers were going to have to fend for themselves!"

He was not going to spend another horrible Christmas holiday alone in his apartment, but instead, he was going to travel to New England for a holiday retreat and his dream was to stand on a field of undisturbed snow, and deeply breathe in the crisp, winter air. Humphrey finished the pre-Christmas series of strips with a frame of Egbert's friends, dropping him off at the train station. All of them, still in shock, while sadly saying goodbye to their friend. Humphrey left the cartoon storyline wide open with the cartoon character alone in front of the ominous, gloomy train station platform, train ticket in his hand, a trip looming, his one lonely suitcase sitting next to him.

Will Egbert and Humphrey actually have the courage to go through with it? The master creator pondered the next strip in his mind. After all, for an introvert, venturing outside in the world can be a frightening and perhaps even a dangerous experience.

A few seconds after Humphrey completed the drawing and dialogue for the strip, in fact, he literally had just laid his pencil down, and the telephone rang. He seldom received calls from anyone other than business related conversations, and glancing at his watch, he felt it was too early for a business call. It seemed strange for the telephone to ring.

Humphrey picked the telephone up on the second ring.

"Hello, Humphrey J. Whitehouse, speaking."

"Humphrey, James Richardson here. How are you?" Humphrey relaxed; his radar went down since James Richardson was a salesman who worked for his publishing company. James Richardson provided marketing and sales services for Humphrey through the publishing company.

"I am fine, James. It is very nice to hear from you. How are you doing? It has been a long time since I have heard from you."

"Yes, it has been. I do apologize for that, but you know how things always become so crazy sometimes. I do have some new promotional ideas to run by you, some new marketing angles. However, that is not the actual reason that I called today. Look, Humphrey, I think that I already know the answer to this, but I need to ask you, anyway."

"Please do, James. How can I help you?"

"Well, Humphrey, I know how you enjoy being by

yourself, you know, working alone, living alone, but in a month or so, right before the holidays, we have a large conference and sales convention scheduled up in New England. The event will be in Massachusetts, just outside of Boston. Big hotel, resort, the works, and wow, if you would come and make an appearance as the headline guest, you know, a meet and greet, sign some books, autograph your strips, speak a little about creativity and about how a budding artist might try to break in with our company. Honestly, it might just make my career!"

Humphrey carefully listened to James, but did not know how to answer him.

In fact, there was little time to speak, because James launched back into a sales pitch, "All expenses paid by the company, of course, the finest meals, all the best wine available, top shelf drinks, hotel rooms, and transportation with all of it on us. New England at Christmas time, fields of undisturbed snow, cold and crisp air! It will be beautiful!"

Humphrey felt a ripple of shock rolling down his spine. It seemed very strange on the heels of his completion of that first cartoon strip to receive an invitation for a trip. A trip that was virtually identical to what he had just conceived a few minutes earlier!

The shocked cartoonist recovered a little and stumbled over a few words, "Well, I, ah, ah, James, I must say that I will certainly think about it. What are the dates? Why me?"

James was oblivious to the questions posed by Humphrey. Instead, he wailed onward with his sales pitch.

He must have been surprised that Humphrey had allowed him to continue this far, because he worked in a little sympathy angle to his cause, "This self-publishing craze is making a huge dent in our business, if I can feature you and your phenomenal success it would be a huge bonanza. Well, it just makes sense to have you appear. I know that people close to you would be shocked for you to step out a bit, but to be honest—I need the boost, Humphrey. It has been a bit rough the last six months or so. I am trying to sign some new blood! Novelists, short stories, cartoonists, anyone who writes quality material. It is hard to find these days."

Humphrey was vaguely listening to the sales pitch from James, but in all honesty, he did not hear much of what he was actually saying. Humphrey was trying hard to convince himself that this was all just a strange coincidence. The fact that he had just completed a series of strips that paralleled this same situation with his own character, was just a coincidence.

"You did not hear it from me, but our editors are a bunch of old jackasses. They try to keep it under wraps that they rejected four manuscripts this year, which went on to be self-published bestsellers. In fact, one of them is gonna be made into a friggin' movie! It is time for these old bastards to pull their heads out of their asses"

Humphrey's mind returned to reality and in order to recover from the shock of the conversation, he rather curtly cut the telephone call short, "James, I will give it some thought. Thank you for the invitation. Please take good care of yourself. Goodbye."

Humphrey slowly hung up the telephone, and he stood there with his hand stuck upon the handset while he continued staring at it for a long time. He still discounted the entire situation as a mere coincidence, just one of those strange things that occur on occasion, still, it was hard not to be slightly amazed when James had made the statement, "Fields of undisturbed snow, cold and crisp air! It will be beautiful!" Those words continued to shock the now very puzzled Humphrey J. Whitehouse. His own words, his own experience. How strange was that conversation? On the other hand, was it merely a wild coincidence?

Slowly, with his hands in his pockets, his head down, Humphrey walked over to his drawing table. He gazed at the strip he just completed and studied it for a long time.

His mood suddenly changed from being pensive to suddenly being adventurous.

He climbed back up on the stool, took out a fresh drawing outline, grabbed a pencil, and in a few minutes, he had the first block drawn. It began with Egbert venturing out of his comfort zone, in a tavern at Christmas time, ordering a glass of fine, top-shelf, single malt Scotch on the rocks. Humphrey went back, redrew the first frame of the cartoon, and instead, he made the drink that Egbert was enjoying, a double. He also drew some dialogue where the novice drinker receives a lecture from the bartender on ruining a fine Scotch by adding ice cubes to the drink, and instead, has the drink prepared neat. His readers will be shocked at the fact that their beloved character was even indulging in an alcoholic beverage, nonetheless that he hurled down a double! Typically, Humphrey allowed Egbert one drink a year, usually a few meager sips from a glass of champagne, which he traditionally sipped on New Year's Eve alone in his lonely apartment. Characteristically, each year, despite taking only a meager sip or two and not even finishing the glass, the final frame of the strip has Egbert spending New Year's Day in bed, hung-over, with an ice pack on his head.

However, in the new world of *Where Reality Begins*, typical, is no longer a word, which is included in the plans.

The next frame of the strip had a beautiful woman asking if the seat next to him is open and Egbert in some type of shock that a woman has even spoken to him, nonetheless, even desires to sit next to him. Humphrey strategically drew the scene to show how all the other seats at the bar were currently unoccupied, except for one, at the far end of the bar, which had a large, rotund man sitting on the last seat, while slumped over his drink and mired in some type of despair. The final frames of the strip, all perfectly captured the spirit of the new direction of the cartoon, with an exchange of some light and airy conversation, followed up with the two characters exchanging warm smiles.

Could it finally be a love for Egbert?

Oh, my goodness, Humphrey was clearly venturing out of his comfort zone now! He sat back on the stool, put his pencil behind his ear, and smiled. It was now amusing to think that for some reason, for just one brief second, he felt as if his strip actually was where "reality begins." Humphrey folded his arms across his chest, removed the pencil, and continued to ponder.

What if?

He pushed back from the stool; he tossed the pencil on the desk and closed the cover to his drawing tablet. It was the Christmas season, there was a local tavern down the street, within walking distance, and he did not feel like cooking, he had a new shirt and a pair of pants that he had bought a few months for an occasion that he, as usual, skipped out on and did not attend.

In all the years that he lived here, despite the close location of the establishment, he never visited the tavern. On the very rare occasions that he ventured out in public, he took a limousine and reserved a special table at an upscale restaurant deep in the suburbs. There, Humphrey would sit in a quiet corner off by himself, and the management of the establishment made sure that no one knew who he was, or even had the opportunity to venture close to his table. Frequenting this local tavern, a tavern so close to his home, was something that he never considered until now. Just as his character Egbert did in the strip; Humphrey remained within a small circle of life.

How strange!

What if?

An hour or two later, there was Mr. Humphrey J. Whitehouse, the creative genius, the perpetual recluse, the elusive loner, sitting at the bar within the local tavern. He was nursing a poured neat double Scotch, a fine, single-malt, the best the tavern had in stock, while randomly glancing at the tavern's menu, when he looked up and took notice of his surroundings. He had only taken a few sips of the Scotch and already, he could feel a slight numbness from the drink taking over his system. Apparently, he and Egbert shared many tendencies, and one of them was that he seldom partook in any alcoholic dalliances.

The tavern was pleasant enough, a slight odor of stale beer lingered in the air, but it now captured the feeling of the season, with some seasonal decorations displayed here and there, and some festive lights draped over the mirror behind the bar, very similar to the same lights of which he drew in his strip.

When his eyes wandered away from the menu, he recovered from the initial impact of the trickle of alcohol flowing through his veins and he looked around the inside of the tavern. While taking keen notice of his surroundings, Humphrey's body rippled with shock when he took notice at the scene unfolding in front of him. Not only were the Christmas lights and other decorations remarkably similar to what he drew in his cartoon strip just a few hours earlier, but sitting at the end of the bar, in the last seat, was a round, plump, balding man! The man was slumping over his drink, massaging the outside of the glass, while pondering where his life was right now.

This so-called coincidence was just a bit too much for Humphrey to take!

Humphrey J. Whitehouse sat back, picked up his drink and this time, he took a long gulp, and he swallowed the remainder of the Scotch contained in the glass as quickly as he could. The harshness of the ripples of alcohol bit at his throat as it went down, the novice drinker had taken on a little more than he could handle, but he did not have time to nurse the ride, or cough, because before he could recover from the impact of the Scotch, another shock wave rolled in.

"Is this seat taken?" A soft and sultry voice asked in a smooth and resonant delivery from behind Humphrey. His spine tingled again, his hair almost stood on end and now he did cough. In fact, he almost tumbled off his seat at the bar.

"Oh my, I am so sorry! I didn't mean to sneak up on you!"

When Humphrey recovered, he managed somehow to stop choking and instead of falling over from shock at how his false reality had begun to take over his actual life, he remarkably steadied himself. The Scotch had now taken full effect. He was feeling quite numb and now was able to, for once, throw some inhibitions aside. He turned around and stared into the eyes of a gorgeous woman. This remarkable woman was tall, statuesque, with long red hair, and a thin face that was gently framing wide eyes, a perfect smile, not at all, unlike, if not exactly the same gorgeous features as to what features that he had drawn on the woman in his cartoon.

At this point, you would think that Humphrey was becoming a little more used to the fact that what he drew seemed as if it actually became a reality. Perhaps he had, or perhaps the Scotch had numbed him sufficiently enough to alter his own reality.

While he gazed upon this gorgeous woman standing right next to him, Humphrey could not help but to think, 'Wow! I wish I had drawn the next frame. I ended the cartoon right here, just a little too soon. There is no next frame! I ended the cartoon with the initial meeting. What happens now?' Gazing at the gorgeous woman who had magically appeared from who-knows-where, now suddenly to appear within his reality, he knew how he wanted the strip to end, but wondered how it really would.

Since he had actually drawn this portion of the meeting, Humphrey possessed more confidence. He sat back, smiled and motioned for the woman to sit next to him, while somewhat casually saying, "Of course, please do. It is my pleasure."

She smiled at Humphrey and pulled the stool out, while speaking in a soft and gentle voice, "Thank you, I was not sure if you were alone or not. I am somewhat surprised at my good fortune at finding such a handsome man alone at the bar." She then looked at Humphrey and caught his gaze as if she was gauging his reaction to the compliment.

"Dianne Logan is my name," now seated, she introduced herself, while she reached out her hand to Humphrey.

The now clearly puzzled artist sat slightly dumbfounded at not only his good fortune and her compliment, but now that Dianne was sitting so close, he was astounded at how closely she resembled the woman he drew in his cartoon strip. Recovering, he stumbled, bumbled, and finally reached out his hand and gently grasped her hand.

"Yes, Dianne. Yes, indeed, it is my sincere pleasure! Ah, Humphrey J. Whitehouse. Yes, that is my name and indeed it is me."

Once he awkwardly introduced himself, a slight tremor of fear overcame Humphrey, because he generally never used his actual name when appearing in public and speaking to complete strangers. He usually had some silly alias that he used, in order to prevent a fervor and a deluge of autograph hounds, novice photographers, fans and other celebrity hounds, from jumping on a rare opportunity to catch the famous recluse out in public.

He sat back and studied Dianne's reaction and much to his surprise, she at first giggled at his stumbling reaction.

She then smiled and softly said, "Nice to meet you, Humphrey. What a lovely name. So, dignified and such an unusually cautious introduction."

Humphrey thought to himself, "Lovely name! Dignified! No one ever thought his name was anything but a dorky and geeky tag. This situation was shaping up to be more than a chance meeting; it was turning out to be extremely interesting. Furthermore, to her credit, there seemed to be no recognition of his fame. She was not a stalker working the angles and she did not jump up out of her seat and scream out, no! You mean *the* Humphrey J. Whitehouse!"

"So, Dianne Logan, what will you be drinking on this fine and captivating evening? Might I be so bold to suggest that you join me in enjoying a fine, single-malt Scotch such as the one that I just finished was? I suggest that we order the drink neat. There is no sense in spoiling fine Scotch with ice. In fact, let's make it a double."

When Worlds Collide

Part 2

From the Seeds of Despair

Thomas O'Flaherty was a rough and tumble man. He grew up tough, fought, and worked hard for what he had in life; he matured into a sturdy man and never forgot the lessons that life taught to him.

The old and difficult streets of Billington, Massachusetts, remained unforgiving. The last time that Thomas checked, he could not find the address of 123 Easy Street anywhere in the telephone book regarding Billington, Massachusetts. Not that he had spent a large amount of time trying to find it, but he was quite sure that the address did not exist.

His parents did the best they could. Their lack of wealth was not from lack of effort or from a lack of dedication. Sometimes, it is what it is in this life. Thomas knew that fact and he loved his parents with all of his heart. Despite his meager circumstances, he knew that his parents loved him and always were trying as hard as they could to provide what they could for their son. Even as a child, he was tough and rough, but inside, he was a gentle and caring soul.

His father worked as a millwright in a local factory, a union man, who earned what he could and who worked every ounce of overtime that came his way. He had his vices; he had his demons, because every Friday after he finished work, he drank every ounce of alcohol that he could afford to swallow, without causing more debt than the family could manage, but there was little doubt that for some reason, he needed to be numb to face life. Mr. O'Flaherty then crawled home every Friday to sleep it off, recover, and then get back out there on Monday to do it all over again. Mrs. O'Flaherty worked typically long retail hours in a food market, in a store located very close to their home, a store within walking distance. Thomas was an only child and by the time that he was ten years old, he already knew the drill.

No one was going to pave the streets with gold for you; therefore, you needed to earn what you have in this life on your own, work hard and, above all, persevere.

He struggled through school, graduated high school on the third attempt. He was never sure if the school just grew tired of him and let him ride, or if he actually earned his diploma.

Perhaps, in reality, it was a combination thereof.

Thomas flirted with joining the military, and then, at the next to the last minute, he changed his mind just before he signed on the dreaded dotted line. Thomas never did well with people telling him what to do, and he had a feeling that the military would not work out too well. He tried to follow his dad into the trades; the union sponsored him, sent him to school, and apprenticed him. He worked his way up, until he made it all the way to a journeyman designation, when a fistfight with a fellow worker forced him to look elsewhere for employment.

Shortly after that incident, his mom died of high blood pressure and a bad heart and his dad, well, he died of an exploded liver and heartbreak over the loss of his beloved wife.

Seeds of despair.

Yet, from the seeds of despair, men such as Thomas O'Flaherty pick themselves up, and they are remarkably resilient. He took a job driving taxicabs; he knew the streets in and around Billington, and in fact, he knew the streets and roadways all the way into Boston, up to the New Hampshire border and all the way down to Connecticut and Rhode Island too.

Fate twists and turns our lives, and it lays out a plan for us. A plan that seems as if we can never alter it, or change, or argue with it and it is mysterious and all encompassing.

While driving his cab one hot summer day, he picked up a rider, not an ordinary ride, a beautiful young lady, who from the first moment their eyes met, each of them knew that fate had worked its magic once again. A year or so later, they were married and the young couple struck out on their own, into life, their hearts filled with love and their eyes full of stars. The newlyweds found a small apartment in his home city, on the third floor of an old walkup apartment house. Mrs. O'Flaherty worked in the local grocery store as a cash register checkout person and Thomas drove his cab, where he worked as many hours as he could and he stayed out of trouble.

They did not have much. The young couple began the rest of their lives in that tiny apartment that was hot in the summer and freezing in the winter. It boasted a small black and white television on a wobbly stand in the corner of the living room, a stereo set to play some records on, a radio to listen to the local broadcast of the ballgames on, and a few pieces of sparse furniture. It was not a luxurious setting by any description, but it was a start, and they loved each other with all of their hearts. Each day, their love grew, and they held onto each other. They often danced together to their favorite songs playing on the old stereo set in the living room of the apartment, just the two of them, dancing with stars in their eyes and the melodies in their hearts.

A year or thereabouts into their marriage, along came the joy of their young lives. A little girl, and they named her for their favorite thing, dancing together in their living room with stars in their eyes. Melody Anne was the name they gave to the little girl, and the baby seemed as if she had stars in her eyes too.

As we often rise with joy from the seeds of despair, sometimes cruel fate intervenes, and to the seeds of despair, we return. Melody Anne woke up very ill one day. At first, the young parents thought it was a virus. The doctor administered some medicine, and the parents watched the situation and treatment very carefully. The baby enjoyed a little rebound, and then a severe relapse, which forced a return to the doctor. When Melody Anne's condition regressed, the doctor instructed the young parents to take some more aggressive steps with the medical treatments and seek more medical opinions. Melody Anne received examinations by a team of specialists, followed by some tests, followed by a hospital stay and more tests. In the meantime, the money dried up, you can only work so much and when the medical insurance coverage ran over, the bills came.

Oftentimes, when life spirals out of control, trouble comes in waves, and this was no exception to that rule. The cab company in which Thomas worked for was sold, first came a lay-off, then Thomas was called back to work, at a reduced wage and with medical insurance no longer provided.

The new owners of the taxicab company were heartless.

Endlessly, every day, the mailbox was full of bills and warning notices for lack of payments and interest added to the initial charges. The young family could no longer afford rent for their tiny apartment and reluctantly, Thomas shelved his pride and admitted that they had to move in with his in-laws. His in-laws did what they could, but they were working people too, and there was only so much they could afford to do.

Finally, a specialized doctor pronounced his final diagnosis of a rare tumor in a precarious location, and he told the family that, "Melody Anne requires a delicate and specialized operation, in order to walk and talk normally and to lead a normal life, or she will eventually become debilitated and her life span will be twenty years or even less."

After hearing the wretched diagnosis, Thomas knew what he had to do.

Free clinics ignored their pleas. The operation was beyond their capabilities, and only the finest doctors could successfully perform this delicate of an operation. The glass jar with the picture of Melody Anne on the container, sitting upon the counter of the grocery store, collected only a few dollar bills, and the church donations dried up, and in the end, in God we trust, and it seems as if all others needed to pay cash. Cold, hard, cash and the lesson that Thomas learned years ago, about free rides, hit home especially hard. Prayers now went unanswered, priests had nothing to offer and the seeds of despair had sprouted more thorns.

It seemed as if God had forgotten the little family.

Yet, Thomas knew.

He would die for his child, he would die for his wife and in his quiet desperation, he knew in one way or another that somehow, he would obtain the money to pay for this operation. The conflicts inside of Thomas were terrible, if his parents were still alive, he knew how bitterly disappointed they would be in him, yet, he knew no other way out right now, and he felt as if he exhausted all of his connections as well as resources. There remained nowhere left to turn.

Except for one option.

Buying a handgun with all the serial numbers, ground off it and with no traceable identity was easy, and the guns were cheap on the mean streets of Billington. It was especially easy for a taxicab driver who knew all the local thugs, all the shady street corners and all the dark alleys, of which these same thugs hung out in and where these types of deals occurred.

On a horribly dreary night in late spring, Thomas O'Flaherty cruised some of the seedier streets of the city, the windshield wipers of his cab slapping time with some light rain that was spitting out of the sky. He had put some whispers out in strategic locations. Now, all he had to do was to find a small-time hood, whose street name of, "Bullet" told you everything that you needed to know about him.

After he parked his cab about three city blocks away from the location of the meeting, Thomas checked the top pocket of his jacket twice to make sure the cash from his daily tips was safe and secure. He just needed to make his way there without an attack or a mugging; he had to make the deal and then hightail it out of this wretched area of the city.

It all seemed like a workable plan.

A cautious walk down a few city blocks, a few turns, a quick walk by a few burned-out storefronts and he was there.

Thomas stood nervously in the rain, in the growing and creeping fog of the night, in front of a dark, deep alley next to an ugly Chinese restaurant, which spewed some greasy odors into the air. A Chinese restaurant with bulletproof glass and an iron gate in the front. Those patrons who were brave enough to eat food from there slipped the cash under the glass and the food came out the same way.

Even though Thomas seldom smoked, his nerves forced him to pull a pack of cigarettes out of his pocket. He lit one and while he waited for the shady seller to arrive, he took a few quick drags. The moistness of the air did not allow the smoke from the cigarette to lift into the night air. Instead, it fell quickly to his feet and mixed in with the rest of the fog.

There in the shadows . . . Thomas waited.

A few city blocks away, in fact, a few blocks south of

where Thomas now stood, in an even seedier side of the old city, strode a man. He was tall, in fact, he was a very large man, and his long legs covered the sidewalks quickly. He moved with a purpose, with a haste that was unusual. Usually, people around these parts of the city staggered or just fell down in the gutters. He moved quickly, and it was not because he was frightened of his surroundings, or of whom, or what, lurked in the dark alleys and doorways of the neighborhood.

No, instead he moved with a purpose, he moved for a cause.

He was dressed all in black, with sharply creased black trousers, a black shirt, and all he wore as extra protection against the weather was a black leather vest. A vest that despite the rain and fog of the evening, he left unbuttoned except for the last button before his waist. On his head was a black hat with a wide brim, which he pulled down close to his ears. However, you could still make out some of his facial features.

On his feet were black, sharp-tipped boots, with metal clips on the edges that made a distinct clicking noise as he walked along the cold sidewalk. A neatly trimmed, black beard framed his handsome face and his facial features were striking, with a trimmed moustache that neatly lined his mouth.

He walked with an air of confidence while he strode along, not speaking or saying a word, nor even acknowledging anyone.

The city never sleeps, and the drug dealers, addicts, hookers, general thugs, and other persons lurking in the night avoided him. One glance and they all could tell that this particular man was not a person of which you determined would be easy prey. No, despite the fact that he was a fish out of water, you just knew that he was not the type of man to "mess with."

You could see that this was a gentleman that was used

to traveling around, and you could easily see that he was comfortable in many different surroundings. The old city and shady neighborhood meant nothing to him. He moved quickly and easily, and the stares and occasional catcalls of those brave enough to call out to him from some dark corner met with no reaction from the quiet stranger.

Oftentimes, no response is the most powerful response.

He had black, piercing eyes. Eyes that focused straight ahead, eyes that did not move or even glance at the many persons who stared at him. His face was void of all expressions; he had no emotions, and an aura of an ominous presence surrounded him.

He was the quiet stranger in the black hat.

"So, do you have the dough? Seventy-five bucks. Let's make this quick there, Irish guy."

"Yeah, seventy-five bucks and you are sure it is clean of numbers and it is in good condition? I am gonna ditch this thing after I do what I have to do."

"Hell yeah, what do you think? You think that I am an asshole or something. Of course, of course, it is all clean and ready to go. You do not get the name of Bullet for selling shitty weapons. C'mon. Move, move, move, here is the gun! Now, give me the dough. It is not good to hang around here for too long."

Thomas slipped the money to Bullet, and the hand-off of the gun occurred in a flash. Thomas looked at it, spun the chambers, eyed the barrel and stuck it in his pant's pocket. It was when they both turned to leave the dark alley next to the Chinese restaurant that they noticed there was a very large man standing at the entrance of the alley, watching them and blocking the exit.

A very, very large man.

The quiet stranger in the black hat had arrived.

The stranger looked around, up and down, then back to the alley, as if he needed to confirm that this was actually the location of his final destination. Satisfied, he moved closer to the front of the dark alley. His huge frame ominously blocked the alleyway exit. His hat, his silence, his presence, all framed by the city streetlights, and the rain and fog, all combined to send shivers down your spine. It seemed as if he was ten feet tall.

"Oh, shit," was all that Thomas could manage to mutter, and without hesitation, he took off and as quick as a flash, he ran past the quiet stranger who did not attempt even to intercept him or even block his path. Their eyes met for a fleeting second and even while running full speed, Thomas felt a shudder go down his spine as he looked into the black eyes of the quiet stranger. Instead, after a passing glance, the quiet stranger spoke not a word, but moved quickly in the direction of Bullet. The quiet stranger in the black hat could have easily reached over and grabbed Thomas, but it seemed as if the fleeing man was not the target of the stranger. It seemed as if he was intent on meeting with Bullet.

"Why ya runnin'? This guy ain't no cop. Dressed like some kind of dude lost in time! He ain't jackshit!" Bullet boldly yelled out as he watched the quiet stranger advance towards him.

The quiet stranger in the black hat still spoke not a single word, but he continued his advance toward Bullet, who now stood his ground and pulled a handgun from underneath his jacket and pointed it towards the quiet stranger.

"Better stop right there, asshole. I do not know who ya big ass is, but I am about to drop ya and leave ya full of bullets."

The quiet stranger did not slow down, and instead, he closed quickly upon Bullet, who waved the gun and warned him once more, "Ya as good as pushin' up daisies!"

The quiet stranger was now within six feet of Bullet. He looked deeply into his eyes, and he finally spoke, "Go, ahead. If you think, you need to, then go ahead and shoot.

The gun will not fire. Squeeze the trigger as many times as you want to because it will not fire."

Bullet laughed aloud, and because he was not actually a killer, just a misguided thug, Bullet pointed the gun at a random location down in the alley, and he confidently squeezed the trigger of the weapon in pure defiance of the prediction of the quiet stranger in the black hat. One squeeze of the trigger and nothing, then another, and another, and just as predicted, the gun failed to fire!

Bullet now stood face-to-face with the largest man he had ever seen, and he stared into his dark and piercing eyes. Eyes that told Bullet he was in a very difficult predicament. The air suddenly turned intensely cold all around them and Bullet shivered from not only fear, but of the sudden drop in temperature. The look of this strange man's eyes was enough to send fear into his heart and shivers down his spine. In desperation, Bullet hurled the useless weapon towards the quiet stranger in the black hat and decided that he would make a break for it when the gun hit the huge man. The stranger casually and effortlessly caught the weapon in the air. Bullet watched in horror as the quiet stranger in the black hat held the handgun in the air and in one powerful motion, he twisted the barrel of the gun over and around as if it were putty in his hands. He then tore the trigger mechanism apart and tossed the now destroyed weapon aside! The quiet stranger reached out and grabbed the stunned and speechless, Bullet in his powerful arms. As Bullet desperately thrashed around in a hopeless attempt to escape the powerful grasp of the ominous stranger, he realized that his feet were now about three feet off the ground! With one powerful toss, the quiet stranger threw Bullet aside as if he was a rag doll.

When Bullet finally finished rolling along the ground, and came to a rest, the quiet stranger stood over him and softly and politely spoke, "Please, give me the money that Thomas paid you for the gun."

Bullet did not take even a second to think about what the quiet stranger said, nor did he argue or resist. He reached in his pocket and promptly handed over the seventy-five dollars.

The stranger took the wad of money, peeled off a bill, and handed it back to the dumbfounded thug.

"Bullet, consider yourself lucky. Here is ten back. Go get a decent meal. Now tomorrow, go to the corner supermarket, apply for the job that your sister has been begging for you to take and clean your life up. Transform from a street punk into a responsible man and take care of your family and yourself too. First, I need to help Thomas and another person, and then I will be back someday to meet with you. If you think that little roll along the ground hurt, then you best heed my warning, or you have yet to experience the pain that will be in store for you."

The quiet stranger in the black hat tipped his hat to Bullet, turned and walked away.

Bullet sat on the ground, his heart pounding in his chest. He was desperate for answers to know who this huge and powerful man was. Bullet called out into the fog of the night, "What are you, some kinda superhero or something? How the hell are you strong enough to twist metal up like that and tear guns apart with your bare hands? How the hell did you know that the gun would not fire and know about my sister and the job at the supermarket? Shit! C'mon man, tell me!"

The quiet stranger did not answer him, nor did he turn around. Bullet still sat there on the ground, his chest pounding, his breaths coming in deep heaves.

The now neutralized thug mumbled to himself as he felt around his body and checked his mouth to make sure he still had all of his teeth, "Damn. Guess that I am lucky. That dude just tossed me as if I was a feather. Who or what in the hell is that guy? Shit! I was just tryin' to make a few bucks!

Bullet sat for a long time, stunned and in shock as he watched and he listened, until the quiet stranger in the black hat disappeared from his vision, he was lost in the rain and fog of the night, and Bullet could no longer hear the click of the metal tips of his boots on the walkway.

When Worlds Collide

Part 3

The Dark Side

Humphrey sat, while deep in thought, on the stool in front of his drawing table. He rubbed his hands together in a display of gleeful preparation and pondered what it was that he was about to draw. Earlier in the day, he had already surprised poor James Richardson, by accepting his invitation for the convention, and told him that for transportation while he was in New England, he required the finest vehicle that was equipped with four-wheel drive that the rental agency stocked. Humphrey's plans included some fun in the snow, and the vehicle would be an essential part of bringing him to where he wanted to go. He was quite sure that he even knocked the smooth-talking salesman right off his feet when he told him another little tidbit. That fact that he required a hotel room for two, because he was bringing a guest!

On the previous evening, on the way back to his high rise from the tavern, the normally reclusive Humphrey shocked the locals in and around the neighborhood, by appearing in public and chatting with the groups of people who were enjoying late night strolls throughout the downtown area. He also stopped and signed autographs outside his high-rise building.

Oh yes, he also had a new and gorgeous girlfriend. A

certain beautiful young lady named Dianne Logan on his arm.

Life had surely changed in a few short days for Humphrey J. Whitehouse. He remained amazed and stunned at how whatever he seemed to draw on his cartoon strip came to be a reality in his life, and he was not quite sure how to deal with all of it. Something deep inside of him still told him it was all a coincidence, but then again, there was the appearance of Dianne in his life, as well as that man at the end of the bar. The man who appeared in real life exactly as he had drawn him in his cartoon strip! Humphrey had no explanation for all of this. Not to mention the words of James, as well as his invitation.

The cartoonist normally worked weeks in advance, and the first of his "new era" strips arrived earlier this morning on the desk of his editor, and then to the publisher's desk too. As predicted, there were many questions, comments and to a certain extent, some shock at the change in direction of Egbert and his lifestyle within, *Where Reality Begins.*

Humphrey defended his new ideas rather forcibly, he knew in his heart that it was time, he had grown stale, bored, and complacent with his work, as well as his own life and even though the popularity of the strip did not indicate it, he knew that a change of direction was in order. When his agent called, and told him that this "new era" of Egbert was going to risk a loss of some of his readership and some syndication losses too, Humphrey still held the line.

Change is always hard, but in many cases, it is necessary. Humphrey's soul now cried out for change, and as the creator and the owner of all the copyrights, he ultimately controlled his own work. The truth of the matter was that he could pack up his pencils now, never draw another strip, and live easily for the rest of his life on the royalties and his accumulated wealth. He had more money right now than he knew what to do with, but that was not the point. When you are a creative artist, your soul is never satisfied unless you are creating; you work until you feel as if you have nothing left to say.

Dianne Logan was magical. Within one night, just as Egbert in his make-believe world had done, Dianne and Humphrey had fallen deeply in love. Not only was she a gorgeous and gentle creature, but also when she finally realized who Humphrey was, the truth of his fame and identity had no impact on their relationship. Once again, his strip became a reality. Humphrey had drawn how Egbert had found true love in his subsequent strips and Humphrey now was convinced that this was the case for him and Dianne too.

Now, he sat poised over his drawing table, and the direction that he wanted to bring Egbert in was somewhat startling, even to his creator.

In the follow-up strips, Humphrey had drawn Egbert on his Christmas vacation, driving around in an elaborate four-wheel-drive vehicle, touring the sights with his new girlfriend on his arm, and the newest idea that Humphrey had was somewhat puzzling. It bordered upon a power trip of some sort. You see, Humphrey felt as if he could now draw what he wanted to happen for Egbert and for him too!

Humphrey leaned in and he feverishly began to draw the new cartoon strip. He had no apprehension and no doubts as he threw caution to the wind and he was going to test his new power and abilities to manipulate and control the real world.

Not only was his request of James for a four-wheel-drive vehicle a test, but now, Humphrey took the test of reality to another level.

In the strip, Egbert was going to stop at a liquor store, and buy a bottle of expensive champagne for him and his girlfriend to enjoy in their hotel room at a glorious New

England ski resort. While he was purchasing the champagne, Egbert would indulge in something that was also completely out of his normal personality. He was going to purchase a lottery ticket and gamble. Egbert purchased one of those mega-jackpot lottery tickets, and that fact was what puzzled Humphrey the most. Egbert in his fictitious world needed the money, but in the real world, Humphrey did not. This was more sampling of reality, to see if he really had the power to manipulate everything and anything.

Had Humphrey somehow actually arrived on the edge of where reality really begins?

The master cartoonist laid his pencil down, leaving the strip dangling with Egbert studying the ticket, while his new gal smiled at him and they enjoyed together what was potentially his good fortune.

On the other hand, was it?

Perhaps all of this now had toppled over the edge, and during the last few amazing days, the normally placid and unassuming Humphrey J. Whitehouse had inched continuously closer to falling over to the dark side. Or perhaps he had already fallen, and he just needed to realize it.

When Worlds Collide

Part 4

An Old Adage

The waiting line at the event to meet and greet the great cartoonist, Mr. Humphrey J. Whitehouse seemingly stretched as far as the eye could see.

Maybe even further. Dianne Logan stood on the sideline, next to the table where Humphrey met his adoring fans, and she was beaming; even she had no idea until now of the amazing popularity of her new beau. Standing next to her was the frustrated salesman, Mr. James Richardson, and he too was ecstatic at the incredible outpouring and turnout for the event. He was making connections and obtaining sales leads beyond his wildest dreams!

This was a monumental event, actually, a historic event. The normally inaccessible and reclusive, Humphrey J. Whitehouse, suddenly accessible to his multitudes of affectionate fans. Both his adoring fans, and the media, stumbled over one another in an attempt to provide press coverage of the appearance of Humphrey at the occasion.

Standing off to the side of the table where Humphrey sat greeting his adoring fans, in a solitary space where very few people noticed him, stood a man. This man was watching the situation very carefully, and he remained intently focused upon the scene where Humphrey met his fans. His lean, tall, and muscular frame remained slightly concealed in the poor lighting of the obscure location. The man was dressed all in black; he wore a black vest covering a perfectly pressed black buttoned-up shirt, and his sharply creased black trousers had no ripples or wrinkles. On his head, he wore a wide-brimmed black hat, pulled down so that his facial features were barely visible.

There, watching in the shadows, was the quiet stranger in the black hat.

A few persons noticed him, mostly women glanced his way. The dark stranger's handsome appearance was a magnet, and even in the dim light and with his hat pulled down, his features and large size were striking and very captivating.

Women walking by would glance his way, spot him standing there and they could not help but to smile and mumble, "Hello." All conversations went unanswered and were to no avail; the man did not answer them or even acknowledge their greetings.

After many hours of unprecedented interaction with his fans, Humphrey's agent decided that enough was enough; after all, you cannot give away too much!

Everything nowadays has a price attached to it.

Everything. Some prices are clear and concise with tags and paid for with cash or credit, others, well there are other types of prices that we have to pay. . ..

When the meet and greet for the world-famous cartoonist finally ended, Humphrey's agent swooped in alongside Mr. Richardson, and with the gorgeous Dianne Logan on his arm, Humphrey turned and waved goodbye to his adoring fans. He was now on top of the world, in control, powerful, the world ostensibly and remarkably, all controlled by the whim of whatever he wanted to draw, in order to create his own reality. He did not worry about the apparently supernatural influences of all of this because he was just going to enjoy it. In fact, he wondered why he had waited this long to change his life!

Humphrey, Dianne, and the cartoonist's protective entourage proceeded to exit the convention hall, and when they turned down a hallway, the group stepped right into the path of the quiet stranger in the black hat.

Their eyes met, and Humphrey felt a shiver go down his spine while he stared into the dark eyes of the mysterious stranger. He had never seen such eyes, or felt such a force, a force, which felt as if this stranger could see and feel what it was that Humphrey was feeling inside of him. His soul revealed, his deepest thoughts now exposed, and Humphrey felt as if the stranger had revealed and torn away all of his darkest and innermost secrets from the deepest recesses of his mind. Humphrey let out with a little gasp and held Dianne's arm tightly, as if the ripples of shock from the meeting of their eyes had caused him to reel in horror.

Dianne sensed her lover's shock, and she quickly asked, "Humphrey, what is it? Are you okay?"

The cartoonist stalled and recovered as he stammered, "I am, ah, ah, I think. . .."

All of these feelings within seconds, all due to the stranger's powerful gaze. Immediately, the agent and Mr. Richardson pushed ahead of Humphrey and Dianne. They covered and provided interference for their precious celebrity.

Humphrey's agent spoke out to the quiet stranger, "Please, please, please, the event has concluded. We are very sorry, but Mr. Whitehouse is now leaving, please no additional autographs and no photographs."

The quiet stranger in the black hat did not answer them, nor did he even react, and the agent as well as Mr. Richardson, stalled in their efforts when they too, met the ominous gaze of the quiet stranger.

They at first felt a sense of danger from the dark and immense man standing in their path, and the agent almost called out for the security force for the convention hall to intervene, fearing a threatening and volatile situation was materializing.

However, before they could react, the quiet stranger gazed down upon the smaller men and quietly spoke in a deep and melodious voice, “His fame means nothing to me, and it should not mean much to you, either. Fame is not a true measure of a person’s worth in this world.”

The quiet stranger turned to the startled and somewhat perplexed Humphrey and simply said, “I know what you have drawn is your inner hope for where your reality will actually begin. Be assured that when the time comes, it will be a reality, and you will do what you know in your heart is correct. Humphrey, you are a good man, please, you must be careful of the power to control what you perceive to be everything and anything, and understand that your influence counts with many. It just might be the old adage of be careful of what you wish for.

The quiet stranger in the black hat tipped his hat, turned, and walked briskly away.

Dianne was puzzled. She leaned over, and while speaking just above a whisper, Dianne asked Humphrey, “What was that all about? Do you know that man? What did he mean about your power to control everything and anything? How strange a message! How captivating a man! He was dressed so perfectly, yet, he seems to be from a time so long ago.”

Humphrey slowly recovered, yet he remained astounded. And all he could manage to do was to mumble, “I have no idea, Dianne. No idea. It was all so strange, but as of late, so many things are inexplicable. I have no idea who he is, or what he might be. I can assure you that I never met the man before. He certainly is a large man and dressed so impeccably. Almost as if, he is lost in time. Very strange indeed. Perhaps, he is a misguided fan. I do not know.”

In silence and in awe, they all stood there watching and

listening, until they could no longer hear the click of the metal tips of his boots upon the floor and he disappeared from their view.

When Worlds Collide

Part 5

Desperation

Thomas O'Flaherty stood on the street corner, hiding in the shadows, being aware of the glow of any streetlights, while he nervously watched the front entrance to the liquor store. Despite the chill of the evening, his palms and his armpits were dripping with sweat and he wiped the sweat from his forehead with his hand. The heavy woolen hat that he wore to cover most of his head and helped to conceal his appearance transformed him into a sweat machine.

He reached in his pocket to make sure the gun was still there. Thomas had watched the handsome couple park in front of the liquor store; they were going to stop for some liquid enjoyment to make their night into a celebration. Thomas was now going to, unfortunately, interrupt that joy. He carefully watched them while they parked, made a quick dash into the store, and his plan immediately changed before his eyes. Holding up and stealing the cash from the liquor store's cash register was his original thought, but now, he thought how this had all evolved into where he could net all the money that he required in one quick shot, by performing one evil deed.

The young couple were striking. They were well dressed, a beautiful woman in a fur coat, and a woman who most likely was wearing expensive jewelry for their night out on the town. The man, some type of high roller, was wearing an expensive suit, and Thomas caught the glimmer of a watch on his wrist that Thomas was sure was worth a fortune. Then above all, there was the vehicle that they were driving, which was a very expensive vehicle. The vehicle was a top of the line, four-wheel-drive-vehicle. Oh my, he knew that was the golden pay-off. He knew exactly where to drive the automobile to and he could be there within minutes! He knew where the operation was in a dirty old junkyard, located on a dark side street, where a mobster fenced vehicles, switched out numbers, changed and transformed them within hours. The mobster asked no questions, the local mob protected him and he paid cash too.

It was a good plan, and he had no doubt that the payoff for his secondary plan far outweighed what could be a meager haul from the cash register. Not to mention that this would be a cleaner and quicker crime to commit. Going inside the store could become messy.

The fancy couple had even parked the car in just the right spot, away from the streetlights, and the dark and dreary night provided more darkness and cover. They were novices to the evil ways of the mean old city.

Thomas thought about how he could pull the hat down and hide his face; it would take just two minutes, no more and no less.

He had to do this. No one will be hurt, insurance will pay them back, they seemed like nice people, but he would die for his wife and for his child, and tonight, he was prepared to do so.

Humphrey J. Whitehouse and Dianne Logan exited the liquor store, arm-in-arm, smiling, chatting about their success, now laughing at and dismissing the odd and disturbing stranger they had met in the convention hall as some random eccentric man. They now surmised that he was merely an overzealous fan who meant no real harm, but somehow had moved in his mind from the real world, to where worlds collide within Humphrey's cartoon world.

Dianne commented how his manner of dress seemed as if he mimicked some cartoon character superhero that he had no doubt created within his mind! They both agreed he was just a strange man who had slipped from the cartoon world and dangled over the edge of reality.

In his free hand, Humphrey now held a bottle of the most expensive champagne that the corner store sold, and in his front pocket was a lottery ticket for the mega-jackpot prize drawing for tomorrow. They laughed and chuckled as he led Dianne around the car to let her into the passenger's side, when a large and powerful man suddenly pulled Humphrey from behind, spun the cartoonist around and almost knocked him to the ground.

"ON THE GROUND. THE BOTH OF YOU! I NEED THE CAR KEYS AND YOUR WALLET. YOU HONEY, I NEED THOSE PEARLS, YOUR FUR COAT! ALL OF IT!" QUICK, QUICK, QUICK! OR I SWEAR THAT I WILL SHOOT!" Thomas O'Flaherty screamed as he cocked the trigger, and the audible click of the weapon was all that Humphrey needed to hear in order to cooperate.

The bottle of champagne flew out of his hand and it crashed to the ground, spewing broken glass and the bubbly liquid in all directions.

Humphrey was a new man, no longer was Humphrey a solitary recluse, a meek and mellow man, and he, too, would die for the woman that he loved.

The cartoonist faced cold reality. He leaned over and protected Dianne with his own body and shielded his love from any bullets.

Humphrey shouted, "Please, I will give you anything and everything, don't shoot! Everything is yours . . . here! Leave her alone, please shoot me and kill me first, but leave this precious woman alone! I have money! I have lots and lots of money!"

Humphrey pleaded, while he was handing everything over to Thomas. The novice crook held the weapon out in front of him, only inches away from the two victims.

Dianne sobbed and trembled as she removed her jewelry and handed it over to Thomas, who screamed for them to, "Move quicker!"

"The gun will not fire," a deep, low voice came out of the night. Along with the voice, the loud, distinctive, audible clicks of metal tips of boots moving along a sidewalk rang through the night air.

When Thomas heard the voice, he panicked at the appearance of a witness. Suddenly, his plan had gone wrong! Thomas violently pushed Humphrey aside, and the cartoonist tumbled backwards while Thomas grabbed Dianne and spun her around. Thomas held the gun to her head while the poor woman screamed in terror. Humphrey jumped to his feet and was about to rush in and try to save his precious Dianne when the words of Thomas and his actions caused Humphrey to freeze in his footsteps.

"BACK OFF OR I BLOW HER PRETTY HEAD OFF!" Thomas screamed and as he stared in the direction of the man moving towards them, his mouth dropped, and despite the horrible circumstances, his spine tingled even more.

"You! The big guy in the black hat . . . you are the man . . . you were there . . . on the night when I bought the gun! You were there in the alley," Thomas said as he stared into the eyes of the quiet stranger in the black hat.

Humphrey also recognized the quiet stranger, and he screamed and said, "Yes! We met you! You were there in the convention hall today! Please, please, help us. Call the police. Help us!"

The quiet stranger in the black hat shook his head and softly asked, "Why are you afraid? We do not require the services of the police. I have already told you that the gun will not fire. Thomas, I can see into your heart and I know that you love your family with all of your heart and soul. Mr. Thomas O'Flaherty, have faith in my words. Point the gun at me, pull the trigger and you will see that it will not fire."

The quiet stranger stopped a few feet away and stared into the horrified eyes of Thomas O'Flaherty.

The immense stranger tilted his head down to better meet the want-to-be-thief's eyes and explained, "You are not a killer. You are just desperate. A man who feels as if he is out of options. Your prayers and the prayers of all the others invoked action. Despite your doubts, I am here. I assure you that the prayers did not go unheard. We are never without hope. Ever. Go ahead, if you feel you need to believe that what I say is the truth, then go ahead and pull the trigger."

The stranger stepped forward again, and he now was standing directly in front of Thomas while he remained locked on the desperate father's eyes. Thomas shook and trembled, and he let go of Dianne, who ran to Humphrey and fell into his arms.

"All of you! Please, back off! You, the big guy in the hat, I do not know who the hell you are, what you mean by answered prayers, how you know me, why you were there on that night in the alley, and why you are here now, but I swear, I will shoot. You are wrong. The gun is brand new, and it will fire. Now, back off!" Thomas shouted and to prove a point and create a diversion to plan his escape route, Thomas held the gun out and pointed the gun sight and barrel to a random location in a far-off gutter of the street. A void location in this weary world. He pulled the trigger and . . . nothing.

He frantically pulled the trigger again, and nothing. One more time, and once again, nothing.

Now Thomas was clearly out of options.

The quiet stranger in the black hat held his right hand out and indicated for Thomas to hand over the gun. In his left hand, he held a wad of dollar bills.

The quiet stranger explained, "I told you that the gun will not fire. Here is sixty-five dollars returned from Bullet for the sale of the gun. I graciously allowed him to keep ten dollars so that he could purchase a meal that night. This entire episode can end right here and now and it will cost you only ten dollars. You might want to give some money to Humphrey here to repay him for the broken bottle of champagne. No one will be hurt and the rewards that you will benefit from having simple faith will be unimaginable. Have faith, Thomas."

Thomas looked first at the cash in the quiet stranger's hand and then he looked back at the eyes of the quiet stranger in the black hat. Something had changed in a flash. This time, the stranger's gaze was no longer ominous, but it was deeply warm, emotional, and caring. Tears filled Thomas' eyes, his heart that was previously racing and pounding in his chest, now calmed and he knew that somehow this strange man had arrived in order to help him, in his most desperate hour of need.

Perhaps their prayers, as the quiet stranger had just told them, did receive some type of answer. How and from where, Thomas did not know, but he knew the calmness in his heart was real.

Thomas gently reached out and took the money from the quiet stranger in the black hat while handing him the gun.

The quiet stranger gently spoke, "Thomas, in life's most desperate moments, there is always someone who cares, even if you think you have run out of hope. Now, there is a better way, a voice in the wilderness, a light to guide you. We can all forget this rather easily, and all of it is with a purpose. All of you here tonight, needed to learn and share in life's lessons. Please return the items you have taken and pay Humphrey for the lost bottle of champagne."

The quiet stranger turned to Humphrey, and he pointed with his finger and said, "You first imagined it, and then you drew it, now you need to live it. You now know why all the events that you have drawn have become a reality. Because your heart is good and your intentions are pure, then, please, trust your heart. In your heart, you know what to do."

Humphrey instantly knew what the stranger was referring to, and he reached into his pocket, pulled out the lottery ticket and held it out in the air to hand over to Thomas, who without any further hesitation, was already placing the goods that he had stolen on the hood of Humphrey's car.

Somehow, for some reason, trust had taken over all of their hearts.

Humphrey told him while handing over the ticket, "Here, take it. Keep the other money. The champagne means nothing. Please, take the lottery ticket. All I can tell you is that, the ticket is a sure winner. It is a mega-jackpot winner. Please, believe me and trust me, just as you have trusted the stranger in the black hat that we can forget all of this."

Thomas shook his head at the madness of all of this, and even though he now was out of options, and had a certain amount of trust within his heart, he still had some doubts.

He asked Humphrey, "How the hell do you know that? How do I know the police are not on the way right now?"

Humphrey walked over; he reached out and gently placed his hand on Thomas O'Flaherty's shoulder and told him, "There are no police. The ticket is a winner. Because, I know, it is where reality begins and our worlds collide. Whatever has caused you to be so desperate for money, then this will be the answer you need and so much more. Look around, my desperate friend. Do you not see more than just a coincidence here? Your prayers, and to a certain extent, my prayers have also been heard."

Thomas looked around at the three of them. He took the ticket and stuffed it in his pocket and his eyes met the quiet stranger's eyes.

Thomas wiped his eyes of uncontrolled tears and forced an unsure smile, "Thank you. This is all beyond me. I cannot understand what has happened here. I have no idea who you are or who these people are. Innocent people that I was going to steal from and violate their lives for my own desperate cause. Yet, I know you are all here to help me. For some reason, I trust you. I have no choice, but to trust and believe that prayers have sent all of you to me and for some good and kind reason, we met."

While looking under the rim of his hat, the quiet stranger told Thomas, "Go home to your family, Thomas. Tell them you bought a lottery ticket tonight. From now on, know there is a powerful light in the darkness. Above all, always trust in what you feel within your heart."

Thomas nodded, he looked once more at Dianne and Humphrey, he mumbled as to how sorry he was and ran off into the night. Dianne held onto Humphrey. She buried her face in his chest, and she sobbed quietly.

"I have no idea who you are, or how it is that you know what you know, but thank you, dark stranger in the black hat." Humphrey held his woman tightly in his arms while he addressed the stranger. "I have to ask, even if I am better off not knowing, just who are you?"

The quiet stranger in the black hat smiled, and even in the dim light of the lone street light, they could make out his striking features.

His deep, melodious voice resonated through the night, "I am who you want me to be. I think we can safely say that I am someone who trusted that you would do what you knew was already within your heart. I also know how you will draw the ending to all of this. Standing on the edge of a field of undisturbed snow, arm-in-arm, along with your beautiful companion at your side, breathing in the fresh clean air. A new life, a new start, and a refreshed soul. You will touch many lives in powerful and grand ways before you leave this world. All of your talent and all of your love could not remain contained inside of a reclusive shell forever. It would have been such a waste. You will now be happier, knowing that you have a greater purpose than being a cartoonist. You can know great joy because when you needed to the most in your life, you trusted your heart for a worthwhile cause. It will be one of the greatest moments of your life."

He tipped his hat, turned, and walked briskly away. Within minutes, he disappeared into the night, and Dianne and Humphrey could no longer hear the click of the metal tips of his boots along the walkway.

When Worlds Collide

Culmination

"Mr. and Mrs. O'Flaherty, with great joy, I have to tell you that the operation was a resounding success! It was a long procedure. We had four surgeons in there to assist me. Melody Anne has a long recovery time in front of her, a struggle, a little bit of angst, but she is going to be fine. I can tell you with pride in my heart and joy on my lips that she will live a normal and healthy life."

The tears of joy had no limits for the happy parents. No limits, as they held onto one another and sobbed together in their limitless love and in their joy.

As they held each other and hugged while standing in the middle of the hospital waiting room, Thomas looked up and over his wife's shoulder. His eyes scanned the scene, the doctor and nurses smiling and beaming as they shared in the joy of the moment of wonderful news, yet Thomas knew somehow—that he would appear. Where was he? His heart told him to keep looking. Finally, there at the edge of the hallway, just beyond the doorway of the waiting room, Thomas saw him.

There stood the quiet stranger in the black hat.

The two men did not exchange any words. There was no need for them to speak. However, their eyes met once again. Thomas smiled and thanked him with his eyes. The quiet stranger in the black hat smiled too, and he tipped his hat, turned and walked briskly away. Thomas stood there holding his wife as tightly as he could until he could no longer hear the sound of the metal tips of his boots along the hospital hallway.

Alone, in his high-rise penthouse, high above the city, at his drawing board, Humphrey J. Whitehouse worked feverishly.

He drew and drew. Frame after frame. He drew as he never drew before in his life.

First, he drew a series of cartoons, displaying how Egbert won the lottery. Then, he drew how he quit his job, left his friends and sold off everything to move out to the country in New England, in order to live in a cabin in the woods. There, Egbert would live forever more, until the end of time with his lovely girlfriend, who was soon to be his wife. Next, Egbert married, and as he and his new love stood arm-in-arm on the edge of a field of snow, that lay undisturbed in regal beauty, his wife gently whispered that Egbert, the man who previously had no life, now had given new life to this world, and that he was going to be a father.

That is how the magnificent cartoon strip ended. Much to the howl and chagrin of his worldwide fans, Humphrey ended, *Where Reality Begins.*

He felt as if he had nothing left to say. After all, how he drew it would be how he knew it would end.

Humphrey now stood on the edge of the field of undisturbed snow, arm-in-arm with Mrs. Humphrey J. Whitehouse. He did not think that in his entire life, he had ever seen or even imagined such a majestic and wonderful sight. His wife was next to him, gently resting her head on his shoulder. She was captivating in her glowing beauty framed by the backdrop of the most glorious landscape he had ever seen.

Dianne Whitehouse leaned into her husband and gently whispered, "You know, my darling. Now, you need a new mission. Something that you can pass along to your son or your daughter. I think the baby might be a girl. I do not know why I know that, but you know how a mother's intuition is. Maybe, you will do a new strip or even a book. Do you have any ideas?"

Humphrey took a deep breath. He knew deep in his heart why this all happened and he felt assured that he had achieved such a greater purpose than just drawing a humorous cartoon strip for the mutual enjoyment of people. He knew there was so much more to it than just that.

"I think I do, my dear. I think I will teach cartooning in a new school that we will create together. I have a special vision. Perhaps, we will teach art and cartooning in a school within the inner city and provide opportunities for the underprivileged young people of this world. James Richardson is correct because due to greed and evil business methodology, we miss so much hidden talent these days. Then, in between, I have a new fantasy strip in mind, a new character, a mysterious character, a new and exciting venture. I will call it, The Adventures of the Quiet Stranger in the Black Hat."

His wife smiled and said, "I like that. I like that a lot. Do you have any idea of who that man really is?"

"Not really, my love. Perhaps he is not actually real, and he lives on the edge of reality and only exists in our minds. On the other hand, maybe he is an angel, or a superhero, a spirit or a ghost, or a time traveler lost in this world. Who knows? This world is full of mysterious things hidden from our view. Beyond our understanding. Maybe he is all of those things and then some more too. However, I think he comes to people when they need faith and love the most. When all is lost, he arrives, first to teach us, and then to bring us the truth, which we already know, we just have to have the faith to realize. Sometimes, in life's greatest mysteries, we are better off just having faith. We cannot see, or feel, or touch faith, but we can sense it in our hearts. I think it is wonderful to know that faith and true love, in this wild ride we all call life, are the two most wonderful emotions of all."

Clyde Ward turned the key in the door of the store, ending another day, another successful mission completed in his new position of assistant manager of the local Foodworld supermarket.

As he turned to head for his car, he was not surprised to run directly into the path of the quiet stranger in the black hat. Clyde stepped back, and he smiled while gently reaching his hand out to shake the hand of the stranger. Under the rim of his black hat, even in the darkness of the parking lot, Clyde could see as the stranger reciprocated with a placid smile and he gently grasped the hand of the man, formally known on the streets of the old city, as "Bullet."

Clyde told the quiet stranger while he fervently shook his hand, "I always knew that someday, I would see you again and meet you. In fact, you told me that we would meet again, and I knew you would keep your word. I do not know why, but I always knew it would be true. You do not speak too much, but when you do speak, it is always the truth. I need to thank you, for knocking me on my ass, and knocking some sense into me. I guess, in retrospect, my brains must have been in my ass."

The quiet stranger in the black hat did not say a word; he only smiled and nodded his head.

Clyde continued to tell his story, "You tossing me around like a rag doll, woke me up, shook me into reality and allowed me to pursue my dreams. For that—I thank you, quiet stranger. I have no idea who the hell you are, other than a very strong son-of-a-bitch, but you gave me what I needed. Besides, I am enjoying this meeting a whole helluva a lot more than our first one. I decided if you were coming back, then I needed to get my life together, because your next visit was going to be something that I did not want to have to deal with. Sometimes, we all need a swift kick in the ass to get our life in order."

Once again, the quiet stranger did not say a word, but he smiled and nodded.

"Look at me now, an assistant manager of this store. I even have a savings account in a bank! I heard that the cab driver made out well too. His daughter is alive and well and he came into mountains of dough. Something about winning the big jackpot in the mega-lottery. Imagine that shit. What a stroke of fantastic luck for a guy who needed it so badly. Amazing actually, but something tells me ya had a lot to do wid it. Good for him. Geez, it seems as if every cab around the city has his name on the side of them now. Damn, this is all so wonderful, but stranger, I have to ask ya. Can ya tell me before you leave, just who the hell are you?"

The quiet stranger in the black hat stepped back. He stood up tall, towering over Clyde and he tilted his head while whispering, "I am whatever and whoever that you wish me to be. I could be a dream, a figment of your imagination, your guardian angel. However, be assured that I am the truth of which you always knew existed in your heart. I am the edge of reality where reality begins."

He tipped his head, nodded, turned, and walked briskly away.

Clyde stood there watching. He smiled, and he mumbled, "Hey, okay then, thank you for you. That works for me."

He watched for a long time, until the stranger left his view, and disappeared into the night and he could no longer hear the sound of his metal boots upon the pavement.

THE END

Murphy

Part 1

In a City's Dark Alley

Within the big city, there are many cruel twists in fate. Behind the big city lights, the excitement, and the picture postcard photographs, there often is darkness . . . a deep foreboding of sorts. In dark corners, and hidden alleyways of the city there often lies deep sadness, many aspects of life that never seem justified, they never seem to make any sense or shed any happiness upon what on the surface, appears to be a somewhat happy world.

Of all these aspects, the human emotion of loneliness might be the most powerful force of all. Perhaps, it is so powerful, because it is so hard to imagine that in a city of millions of people, full of human activity, with the cars, trucks, and buses whizzing about, and big business deals being conducted that loneliness could even exist at all.

Yet, it does.

Within the confines of an overturned old couch, dumped in a filthy alley of the dirty city street, was where the momma dog had her pups. It was not as if she had much choice. It was warm, dry, and available. Besides, there were no humans around to yell at her, or kick her as they often did to the worn-out stray dog. This was her fourth litter in her young life. She spent her life on the street, confined to these dark alleys, and her daily existence consisted of poking for food in overturned trash cans and licking water from rainwater puddles. There were no cozy snuggles in front of warm fireplaces in the life of this poor stray dog. She was just another statistic within the big city. Stray animals in the big city were always a problem and dog pounds and adoption agencies could only save a small percentage of the stray population.

A tiny percentage.

She was a mixed-breed female dog of quite an uncommon combination of various breeds. Part collie, a little mix of a large terrier of sorts, a retriever or two in there somewhere, but this dog was a smart one. The mixed-breeds often are so very smart.

There, in the confines of the overturned couch, four more stray dogs came into the world. Being the outstanding momma that she was, she took good care of her pups. God gives all mothers, in the human world, and in the animal world, and every world in between, the instincts required for perpetuating life. Momma tended to her pups, fed them her milk, guarded them, and life was safe and stable. Safe until one terrible afternoon when the owner of the building next to the alley finally decided, after some prodding and threats of fines by the local city officials, to clean up the accumulation of trash on his property.

A cleanup crew arrived, first they carried away the couch, then they hauled away mountains of other trash, and in a blaze of shouting, growling and a vain defense by momma dog, the crew chased the small family out of the alley and into the cruel streets. The momma dog did her best, and she carried off and corralled most of her litter, all except one little male pup, who scampered off in the wrong direction and was lost in the shuffle's madness. The little puppy ran and ran, and shortly, he was lost to his momma and his brothers and sisters forever. Lost and now lonely in the maze of the big city. People walking the sidewalk reached down and tried to grab the cute, little puppy but he was too fast for them. Some kind-hearted people kept him out of the danger of the city streets, but eventually the frightened little puppy took refuge in another dark alley. There, without his momma and food or water, he would not last very long.

Yet, maybe not, because of all the pups of the litter, this little puppy inherited his mother's keen mind and intelligence.

Scattered in and amongst all the billions of human beings on this planet, there are many great and powerful minds. Great thinkers, brilliant brains, and scientific minds. Minds that can dissect scientific mysteries and apply mathematical formulas to solve every hidden angle of this amazing world. Despite the efforts of these same great minds of humanity, working as hard as they can to understand all the mysteries of creation, and of this world, there remain many unsolved mysteries. Mysteries that those same great minds can only hope to understand or even think about comprehending. One of the greatest of these mysteries is that despite weighing every angle and endless calculating, the greatest scientists can account for body mass and weight in living creatures, except consistently for one percent of that mass.

Somehow, the formulas always come up one percent short.

Perhaps that mysterious and elusive one percent is the soul of every living creature, human or otherwise. No formula or scientific mind can measure, comprehend, or understand the existence of the mystery of the soul.

Only God knows.

Human minds that do not allow for the existence of God, and a master creator in this world, will always fall short, because faith has to be used, not a scientific formula, to solve some of these mysteries.

It is comforting to know that hidden within parts of those same great mysteries, there are guardians for the souls. Guardians to prevent and offset loneliness, guardians for the weak souls, guardians of all that is good, just, and kind. To preserve the joy, to share in the love, to work endlessly to preserve all of God's creation.

In fact, there are even guardians of the souls for the little, lost puppies.

An extremely large, powerfully built man stood outside on the city street in front of the alley where the little puppy ran off to hide in. It was as if he magically and suddenly appeared. He looked around at his surroundings quickly, as if to determine his location and to ensure that this was actually where he intended to be.

The man standing on the street was dressed all in black. He wore a black vest covering a perfectly pressed, black buttoned-up shirt, and his sharply creased, black trousers had not a single ripple or a wrinkle. There was nothing out of place on this man—not a wrinkle, not a hair on his head, nothing. He was impeccable, immaculate.

His features were dark; he wore on his face a finely trimmed beard, closely framing a perfectly chiseled face, dark, piercing black eyes staring straight ahead, emotionless, expressionless. On his head, he wore a black hat, pulled down to where his facial features were not easily seen, but still visible. On his feet were highly polished black boots, buffed to a mirror shine. If you bent down and looked at them, you could see your reflection in them.

He was the quiet stranger in the black hat.

Two long strides later, found the quiet stranger kneeling down in the alley's front, clapping his hands together, while gently saying, "Over here, Murphy. Come along now. It will be fine now. Do not be afraid, you will never need to be afraid. You are very special. I have chosen you. I have a mission for you, my little friend. A long mission, then another one after that. Come on now."

At first, the little puppy looked over at the quiet stranger with sad eyes and fear in his heart. He cowered away and tried hard to hide. Where were his momma, brothers, and sisters? Yet, when he studied the stranger and heard the kindness in his voice, something deep inside of the little puppy came over him, and suddenly, his fear disappeared. The little pup joyfully ran over and into the arms of the quiet stranger in the black hat. The quiet stranger scooped the little dog up in his arms and he held him tightly.

"Good boy, Murphy. First, we will need to wean you, and then I will feed you and take care of you for a while until you are ready. Then, you will begin your mission."

The little puppy gleefully licked the face of his guardian, and together they disappeared into the maze of humanity within the city.

Mr. Christopher Murphy was a retired plumber. For thirty-five years, he ran his own plumbing business, mostly commercial plumbing missions, in the many large commercial facilities within the big city. He did not make a million dollars, but he got by fairly well. He provided for his wife and earned what most people would say was a comfortable income. Their only son, Christopher Murphy Junior, was a casualty in action in Vietnam. That remained a tragedy that his wife and Mr. Murphy never really recovered from, no matter how hard they tried to overcome it. They rented a large apartment on a busy city street in the far west end of the city. The apartment was large and comfortable, the rent was reasonable, and it was in a decent neighborhood. The apartment fit their needs and their lifestyle, and long ago, the couple agreed that the two of them never desired to own their own home. Mr. Murphy worked too many long hours to tend to a lawn or the maintenance needs of a home. Besides, Mr. and Mrs. Murphy both grew up in the city on busy streets, and the two of them rather enjoyed the sound of the traffic going by outside their window. They also enjoyed the fact that you could walk or take a bus to any location or need that your heart could ever desire.

A year or two earlier, Mrs. Murphy took ill and after a brief battle with a terrible disease, she passed away. Now, Mr. Murphy was alone and a deep, powerful and terrible loneliness crept into his life. He was empty inside his heart and his mind.

Mr. Murphy was in fairly good health. He had a bit of stiffness in his knees and lower back from years of twisting wrenches and fighting pipe wars, but overall, he was in good shape for his age. The old plumber made a habit of walking around the city. He had a car, but he kept it in a garage a few blocks away from the apartment. A garage, which he felt that he paid too much for in monthly rent. Mr. Murphy walked to the bank; he walked to mass at a local Catholic church, to the supermarket, to the corner store for beer, newspapers, and a few cigars.

The old plumber also walked over to a local gin mill on a nearby corner to tip a few beers and share stories with some old-timers in the neighborhood. It helped to chase away some loneliness, but his son and his wife were never far from his thoughts. If he examined his heart, there was pain there, a great deal of sorrow, and a feeling of emptiness. There were no relatives left on either side of their families. They were small families to begin with anyhow, and now that time had progressed, his wife outlived all of her family members and now, Mr. Murphy had too.

It often seems as if all of life is a blur.

Early on an April evening, in the dark shadows of the city streets, nearby a corner outside the apartment where Mr. Murphy lived, a tall, lean, yet powerfully built man, dressed all in black, gently held a little male puppy in his arms.

He smiled as he allowed the little puppy to lick his face. The man then spoke to the puppy, softly and quietly, "It is time, Murphy. I will always be with you and when the time is right, we will meet again for your next mission. Be sure to love him, guide him, and help him overcome loneliness, as only a dog can help to do."

The stranger, dressed in black, set the little puppy down in a nook close to a set of concrete stairs, which led to a basement door in front of the apartment house. He went to walk away and the little puppy whimpered and followed him.

The dark stranger turned around, adjusted the black hat upon his head and smiled at the little puppy, while speaking gently to him, "No, it will be fine, little Murphy. Stay. We will meet again someday. I promise. For now, you have a special mission and if you stay right there, all will be well."

The little puppy was highly intelligent, and he understood what the tall, dark stranger had told him. The little puppy listened carefully. He sat, the little dog tilted his head and cried a little, but he wagged his little tail in response to the instructions from the tall and dark stranger. The tall stranger nodded, tipped his hat. He turned and hurried away.

The little puppy still cried a little as he sat and watched the stranger disappear from his sight.

Murphy

Part 2

The Two Best Friends

It was time to pick up a six-pack of beer and a few cigars. And for Mr. Christopher Murphy, that meant a little jaunt to the corner store to pick up the supplies. He took a few steps out of his door, walked down the main hallway and soon the old plumber had spanned the long front steps of his apartment house and he was on the way to the store.

That is, until; he heard the soft whimpering of a little puppy. Christopher Murphy stopped, and he looked around when he heard the cries of the little pup. He always was a dog lover, but the Murphys never owned a dog. Mrs. Murphy was allergic to dog fur and his wife did not share his sentiments towards canines. He spotted the source of the cries as he eyed a little puppy alone and cowering in the corner, tucked up in the nook above the concrete stairs.

Immediately, there was a certain connection.

"Why, hello, there little puppy. Are you lost? C'mon, it will be okay. C'mon, over here," Mr. Murphy said as he knelt down and tried to coax the puppy over to him. At first, the little puppy remained skittish, he backed off and then gradually, the softness and kindness in Mr. Murphy's voice, combined with the memory of the dark stranger's instructions, and the little puppy ran over to Christopher Murphy, and jumped into his arms. The two of them made the connection and now the special bond was complete.

The little puppy enthusiastically greeted his new friend. Mr. Murphy laughed as the little puppy licked his face and wagged his tail in delight.

"Okay, okay, you are a cutie, all right! No collar, no tags. You look as if you have just left your mother a little too early. My goodness, such a handsome stray you are. I need a friend, I really do, and you look as if you need one too. I think we can be friends together. I will call you, Murphy, yes! Murphy will be your name. That will be perfect! Now, I think that I will have a change of plans. The beer and cigars will have to wait. Instead, let's get off to the pet store for some supplies and a collar and a leash, and some dog food too!"

As the two new best friends made their way towards the corner market, the quiet stranger in the black hat stood watching in an obscure and dark corner within the city streets. The stranger was carefully watching from afar while the scene unfolded. When the little dog and his new companion were both a safe distance away, the stranger was now satisfied, he nodded, smiled and turned to walk briskly away, and in a short time, you could no longer hear the click of his metal boots upon the walkway.

Time moved along and as time tends to do it often moves quicker than anyone ever realizes. Mr. Murphy and his faithful dog, Murphy grew old together. Wherever Christopher Murphy went, his dog went too. Murphy the dog grew to be a strong, handsome dog, with a powerful chest and tireless legs. His keen intelligence made him a wonderful companion to his partner and his faithful devotion soon made Mr. Murphy forget the notion of any lingering effects of loneliness. The two Murphy boys, as the neighborhood was quick to tag them, became famous for their constant companionship as they traveled the small circle of the few city blocks where they lived.

It surely seems as if God created dogs to fill a special void in this world, a void of which humans are incapable of filling. Dogs are loyal, respectful, unselfish, happy, living with a mission to protect, as well as love their human companions without any boundaries. Love without any ties, a love that has no rules or prejudice. Unconditional love provided to flawed humans. If only humans could put egos, as well as pride aside, and love as a dog does. A dog's sole mission in life is to make humans feel better, make them feel loved, to snuggle when no one else cares, to keep everyone warm on cold nights, to look in their human companion's eyes and to ask, "How can I love you more than I do right now? What mission can you give me to make you happy?"

You see, in this life, we all need a mission.

Murphy the dog was a very special dog who now had a special mission. The dog would walk faithfully with Mr. Murphy when he went to the corner store, the market, and when he stopped for a few beers at the corner gin mill.

The dog would listen patiently to his companion's instructions, while he said, "Wait here, Murphy. I will be right out."

The dog would sit and faithfully wait until his friend returned, waiting while watching the traffic and human world go by, greeting those people who knew him and making friends of new ones. The dog was wary of strangers until they proved themselves a friend. No one who had any ill intentions, would ever dream of becoming close to Mr. Murphy. When you proved yourself a friend, then Murphy the dog allowed you into the inner circle. Murphy was friendly, but he had a keen sense of his surroundings and outstanding hearing and vision. It would be a very grave mistake ever to try to break into their apartment or to attempt to inflict any harm upon Mr. Christopher Murphy. Murphy the dog would gladly die in protection of his companion before he would allow any harm to come his way.

The two of them went through life together, sitting upon

the front stoop of the apartment on warm and clear nights, watching the world go by, or walking on errands, or just passing time together; they were inseparable.

Christopher Murphy grew older. He bent over at his waist a little more, his hands quivered and shook, he shuffled his feet along as he moved slower and slower with each passing day, and he became increasingly unsteady on his feet. His hearing failed, and his eyesight grew dim and dark. Mr. Murphy sold his car, gave up the garage, which he paid too much in rent on anyway, and now, the two very faithful friends walked or they rode the bus to wherever the two of them needed to go. Soon, Murphy the dog became not only a companion in life, but he became his friend's eyes and his ears too. Without any training, other than his instincts and keen intelligence, Murphy led his now almost blind friend around on his missions. Mr. Murphy leaned over and held onto his dog and allowed him to guide him along and watch for danger, as well as obstacles.

The two of them had grown old together. In the end, time is the only real enemy that we all have. It marches on endlessly; we cannot outrun it, offset it, or delay it. In the end, time always wins and the perpetual change in our lives come to all of us.

"I must say, officers, that I am very concerned. That is the reason why I decided to call. It is not like Mr. Murphy, not to be active, or not to pick up his mail for so many days in a row. And his dog, Murphy, well, he just barks and barks. I know that dog very well, he knows me, and when I speak to him through the door, he cries and whimpers at me as if he needs my help. I am sure that something terrible has happened to Mr. Murphy and that his dog is trying to tell all of us. The poor man is almost blind. Murphy the dog leads him everywhere. He has no relatives, no friends or family left, only Murphy the dog. He told me just last week that he outlived everyone except for Murphy. The dog is very smart. I dare to say, he is smarter than most humans are," Mrs. Govin, the next-door neighbor to Mr. Murphy, rather haltingly explained the situation to two police officers, as they all stood outside the door to Mr. Murphy's apartment.

One of the officers nodded, and he looked over at his partner who was taking notes, as Mrs. Govin told him her testimony, based on not only experience, but some evidence too. Murphy the dog was now barking incessantly on the other side of the apartment door and whimpering intermittently, it was obvious that the dog was desperately trying to bring something of a rather serious nature to the attention of the humans that he could hear speaking on the other side of the door.

"When was the last time that you saw, or spoke with, Mr. Murphy?" The note-taking officer asked Mrs. Govin.

"At least three days ago, or thereabouts, officer."

"And you say that he does not answer the telephone?"

"That is correct. It just rings and rings and rings, with no answer. I had my husband call while I stood outside the door and listened. I can hear the telephone ringing in Mr. Murphy's apartment, but there is no answer. He is so old now that he does not use answering machines or anything modern like that."

The group looked up as the maintenance manager of the building arrived on the scene, carrying a bundle of keys that he sorted through as he approached the door.

"I have the master key right here," he told the officers, as he displayed one key out of a large ring of companion keys.

The officers nodded and one of them made a motion with his hands and arm in the air to stand away from the door.

He gently knocked on the door.

"Mr. Murphy. Mr. Murphy, it is the police, the building manager, and Mrs. Govin from next door. Are you okay there? Do you require assistance?"

They all listened carefully, but there was no response from Mr. Murphy, only the continual barking from Murphy the dog.

After several repeats of the same inquires with the same response, the note-taking officer looked at his watch to time the entry, he nodded to the maintenance manager to use the key in the door and turned to Mrs. Govin and told her, "Please Mrs. Govin, this might be unpleasant. If you can comfort the dog, it will be very helpful. He obviously knows your voice, but I will ask you to remain here in the hallway."

Mrs. Govin held her hands over her mouth. A few tears appeared in her eyes and she nodded to indicate that she understood.

The key spun inside of the lock and when the apartment door opened, Murphy, the dog, immediately sat down in the hallway of the apartment and he looked over the group entering the apartment. He was indeed very smart and a quick scan with his eyes at the humans, as well as the soft voice of Mrs. Govin, told him that this was the arrival of the assistance that he had been requesting.

Mrs. Govin spoke gently, "It is okay, Murphy. We are here to help. Show us where Mr. Murphy is. . .."

Murphy stood up and ran off in the direction of a rear bedroom, then turned back to the group and barked in an effort to convince the group to follow him. A few steps inside of the apartment by the officers and the distinct odor in the air told them all they needed to know. One of the officers motioned to Mrs. Govin and the maintenance manager to stand back and remain in the hallway, as the other officer followed Murphy, while picking his 2-way radio off his belt holster.

He keyed the microphone and radioed in, "Unit 345 to dispatch. We are going to need a coroner representative here at 1322 Washington Ave, Apartment 216. Better send the morgue wagon too."

Mrs. Govin sobbed gently in the hallway as the manager sought to comfort her. The officers followed Murphy the dog to the rear bedroom where they found Christopher Murphy in his bed; it was obvious that he had passed away a few days ago. While Murphy, the dog, allowed the officers to see what the trouble was, his instincts to guard his precious companion remained strong. He would only allow them so far, and when the officers approached any closer, Murphy rapidly convinced the two police officers that coming too close would be a serious and grave mistake on their part.

Murphy, the dog, had a mission given to him many years ago, and the faithful dog was going to follow that mission to the end.

One of the police officers tried very hard to convince Murphy that they needed to approach his friend, "It is okay, Murphy. You are a good dog. We are your friends."

It was to no avail. Their calm voices and passionate speeches, as well as other techniques were not working, and when the two officers realized that their efforts were futile, one of the officers picked his radio off his belt and radioed in the latest development.

"Unit 345 to dispatch. We are going to need animal control here at this location. The pet dog of the deceased is doing his job and he will not allow us to approach the body."

Two animal control officers carefully placed the now drugged, comatose, and limp body of Murphy the dog into the rear of the animal control wagon. They attached a small collar and leash around the dog, and then they gently placed him on a soft pad inside of a special holding compartment.

"Should we lash him down with a strap or put him in one of the cages, instead of just setting him on this pad?" One of the officers asked his partner, who was the lead officer on the patrol.

"Nah. Please, he will be asleep for a week with the kinda' drugs that we shot him up with in there. Besides, this low box and pad are soft and he will sleep tightly and not move around too much back here. Just gonna clip the end of the leash, to this here hook and it will all be well. He ain't going anywhere. I have been doin' this for almost twenty years now and I never saw a more fearless dog that took that combination of drugs to bring him down. I shot more needles in his ass than I ever did for any animal. He for sure, ain't no ordinary run-of-the-mill dog."

The other officer nodded as he double-checked Murphy and closed the door to the wagon.

He agreed with his partner, "No doubt on that one. It was a monumental battle for sure. That is one special dog, who loved that old man with all of his heart. Damn sure did. It is a shame cuz he is a beautiful dog. The cops told me that the old guy had no relatives. An old dog like this one, he is a big dog and people don't ordinarily adopt big, old, dogs too often, even if he is beautiful. Most likely, he ain't gonna find no adopters. Might be a week, maybe two at the most, and he will join the old guy and he will return to this world, as some glue in a bottle."

Murphy

Part 3

On the Sixteenth Floor

On the sixteenth floor, in apartment 16H of the city projects residential high-rise building, a fourteen-year-old young man with the name of Calvin Wilson sat by an open window in his bedroom. The window only opened about halfway, but it was just barely open enough to allow some air to filter into the room. From here, Calvin could hear the noises of the city life echoing up into the air to where he sat high above the madness of the old city. This was a very small bedroom, contained within a cramped apartment. Two small bedrooms, a kitchen with a small cooker within a room that was barely large enough for a refrigerator, and a small table that squeezed in two chairs. There was a living room, or a room of which its intention was to be a living room, but in reality, it was only large enough to hold an undersized sofa, a coffee table and an old television on a rolling stand. The apartment was stifling in the summer and freezing in the winter, and its cramped quarters could be somewhat maddening. The government representatives, when they came to inspect the facilities to continue to allow the subsidized rent checks to flow to the building's operators and owners, looked the other way at the leaky roofs, the boilers that did not fire correctly, and they paid no mind to the rats that ran around in the basement and garbage pits. They ignored the rats as if they were entitled to live here too, as if they paid rent. When the correct amount of money landed in the designated wallets and pockets, then it seemed as if many deficiencies of the buildings magically disappeared.

Calvin stirred as he strained to hear the sounds of the city below. He felt for the tuning knob of the small radio, which sat next to his window and bed. He tuned the radio dial away from the music that he had been listening to, and carefully tuned the dial up the band; until he heard the sounds of the baseball game come to life through the radio's speaker. Satisfied, he placed the radio on the table and listened to the combination of the city life and the baseball game. He could visualize in his mind's eye what was occurring on both of these fronts, but he could not see them because Calvin Wilson was blind. He had not always been blind. A terrible affliction with Cerebral Palsy had stolen the use of his limbs, stolen his ability to speak clearly, and slowly and painfully, it stole his sight from him.

As the affliction progressed, his world grew dimmer and dimmer. Now, all that remained in his mind were faint memories in the darkness of his mind of what the city streets below him actually were like, and of what was happening on the field with the play-by-play announcer's description of the action in the baseball game on the radio.

Sometimes, he wished that he had been blind from birth and never had the ability to see anything. Then his visions would be empty and the longing in his heart to see again would not be so painful, so cruel and so heartless. Other times, he was thankful for the time that he could see, the time that he had, and now he kept those visions deep within his mind forever.

Calvin did not move around well, his palsied limbs were not cooperative, and that fact, combined with his lack of vision, made moving about to be very difficult. His mother worked long hours in a local dry-cleaning store on a city corner, not too far away from the projects. She was doing her best to make ends meet. He never knew his father. He left shortly after Calvin was born, and about the time, the doctors confirmed that Calvin was a victim of Cerebral Palsy.

No one ever heard from him again.

Calvin attended a special school. He obtained medical care from low or no-cost clinics, and he did the best that he could to offset the terrible loneliness that had become his life. Music was a love of his, and when the baseball games were not on the radio, or it was the off-season for baseball, then music would be playing on the radio. He tapped his palsied limbs to the beats and danced alone in his room as best he could. Calvin loved all types of music and he vowed to dance and sing to the music as long as he could until the affliction stole those abilities from him too and he would be in a wheelchair or some type of other confines.

He often wished that he could have one of the new modern types of players that he had heard advertised on the radio and the television. The description of these devices had such appeal to him. Calvin could put the earpieces in his ears and listen to his music in that manner. It was an unrealistic desire, because even if his mother could afford to purchase one of the players, he would have no way to load music or even manipulate the tiny buttons. Besides, if he ventured too far away in the neighborhood or even sat on the front steps with a new music player of that type, it would only last a few minutes before one of the neighborhood thugs stole it from him anyhow.

It was summer now, and it was the middle of baseball season. Therefore, Calvin sat at his lonely post listening to the game and the buzz of the city, waiting for his mother to return home from work. Other than his mother, Calvin had no one in his life. He was another victim of loneliness, with no friends and he had no companions, unless you could count the baseball announcers broadcasting the game.

In another part of the city, far below where Calvin sat and listened to the noises within his own confining world, a very special dog named Murphy with an iron will and a vision of a mission locked in his mind, struggled to his feet in the rear of the animal control wagon. A wagon that was slowly working its way to drop Murphy off to what was going to be a slow and painful march towards a bitter end.

An end, of which Murphy the dog knew that he was not going to be a part of, because it was not yet his time.

The powerful drugs that the animal control officers used to subdue him and capture him still lingered in his body and his mind, but Murphy shook them off as best he could. Murphy shook his head and then shook his body to regain his footing and his composure, and to manage his unsteadiness in the wobbling truck, while it bounced along the city streets. The lead officer's predictions of how the drugs would make him sleep for a week did not account for the fact that Murphy was a very different dog. This was a dog, motivated by a power given to him that most humans might never understand.

Murphy shook his body harder and harder and then he rolled around on the mat, while with his paws he pulled and tugged at the collar and leash that hung around his neck.

Realizing that the leash was the weakest bond, the powerful dog set his sharp teeth and an iron will to work on the leather. Murphy attacked the leash vigorously, and he cut, tugged and pulled at the leather tether until it finally broke loose.

"Well, let's park here, close to the front door of the building. That dog weighs a few pounds and to carry him a long way is not what I want to do on the last stop of the day," the lead officer told his partner, who nodded in agreement with his fellow officer.

Across the street from the animal shelter, standing on a

street corner, while carefully watching the animal control wagon pull into the front of the facility, stood the quiet stranger in the black hat. He stood silently and rather ominously, his dark piercing eyes carefully watching the two officers as they made their way to the rear doors of the truck. He said not a single word to any pedestrians that passed by whenever they stopped and stared at the very large man in his striking attire, with his black hat pulled down tightly upon his head.

The lead officer pulled open the rear door to the wagon and before the two officers could even react, Murphy the dog jumped out of the open doors. While the two officers stood there dumbfounded, Murphy ran and darted away, quickly making his way through the parking lot of the animal shelter and out into the city streets.

"DAMN! THAT DOG! HOW THE HELL IS HE AWAKE? HOW THE HELL DID HE GET LOOSE?" The lead officer screamed as he hung onto the handle of the wagon's door and tried hard to catch his breath at the shock of what just happened.

His partner helped to steady the lead officer while he mumbled, "Ya know, sumthin? You were right when ya said that ain't no ordinary dog."

The lead officer shook his head and mumbled, "This for sure, is gonna look bad on our report."

Murphy the dog tore off through the maze of humanity migrating along the busy city streets. The dog darted and maneuvered his way along, and despite the efforts of many people to corral him or stop him, when they spotted the speeding dog sporting a collar and dragging a leash behind him, their efforts were futile.

Murphy the dog had a mission, but the trouble was that he was not exactly sure of what that mission was going to be at this point. The dog ran along furiously until he finally tired out and the exhausted dog found a quiet nook in a corner of a restaurant's parking lot. There, the dog took a moment to lie down on a cool patch of grass and he panted and recovered from his escape. Murphy looked around and around, and his keen mind knew that the next obstacle that he would need to avoid, would be that same animal control wagon and the two officers that were most likely, right now, patrolling the streets in an effort to find him. While struggling to his feet, Murphy heard a voice from off in the distance that was calling his name. Murphy stood and listened cautiously as the voice of the quiet stranger in the black hat repeatedly called out his name. From somewhere deep in the recess of his memories he knew that voice. He tilted his head, and he listened carefully to the stranger's words as he watched the large man approach him.

"It is okay, Murphy. You are a good dog and you have done very well, my old friend. I told you that we would meet again, and you have been true to your mission. It is now time to eat and relax before we start your next mission."

Murphy at first, backed up and assumed a defensive posture when the quiet stranger came closer, but then the memories in his mind became stronger and he knew that this was his long-lost friend, his savior of sorts, his guide and his first human companion. He ran up to the quiet stranger in the black hat and warmly greeted his old friend as the two embraced, and together, they shared a special moment of reunion.

The next morning, a very unusual duo made their way along the city streets. The usual bustle of the city consisted of many people, yet, somehow, this duo stood out of the crowd. Pedestrians stopped and stared as they noticed a man dressed all in black, with sharply creased black trousers, a black shirt covered by a black leather vest that he left unbuttoned, except for the last button before his waist. On his head was a black hat with a wide brim, which he pulled down close to his ears, but you could still make out some of his facial features.

On his feet were black, sharp-tipped boots, with metal clips on the edges that made a distinct clicking noise as he walked along the cold sidewalk. The large man walked with an air of confidence as he strode along. Everyone who noticed him could tell that this was a gentleman that was used to traveling around, and you could easily see that he was comfortable in many different surroundings. A busy city sidewalk meant nothing to him. He easily navigated the crowds and dodged between the rushes of humanity.

He had black, piercing eyes. Eyes that focused straight ahead, eyes that did not move or even glance at the many pedestrians who stared at him. His face was void of expression; he had no emotions, and an aura of an ominous presence surrounded him.

It seemed as if he had a mission, in which nothing could derail.

Observers could not help but notice how the man, even dressed as perfectly and immaculately as he was, it seemed as if he was from an era of so long ago.

The man moved along at a brisk pace and, walking side-by-side with him and easily keeping pace, was a large, handsome dog that trotted faithfully alongside the man. They quickly paced the many city blocks as they made their way to the destination, which they had in mind. Wherever and whatever that destination might be.

The unusual duo made their way into the more rundown areas of the city. As they passed through the crowds and they walked by a large group of young street-smart toughies hanging out on the porch of a run-down tenement, the two garnered some catcalls and attention.

"Whoa . . . nice hat there, pal! Where ya going so fast? C'mon over here and let's check out those boots! Yeah, we need to take us a closer look at those fancy boots! I bet if we could borrow those boots, we could make cool noises on the sidewalk when we walked too!"

Another member of the group of want–to-be tough guys

called out, as the rest of the gang jumped off the steps, to follow and taunt the quiet stranger in the black hat and Murphy the dog.

"I think ya might be lost. Maybe, you need directions! We can tell you where to go, but it is going to cost you. Nice dog, but the police around here tell us there is a leash law. Mister, you ain't got no leash!"

The group continued on their path, following the unusual pair of friends as the two moved quickly along the city streets. As they walked along, the gang continued to follow. They called out ever more aggressively and they grew frustrated when their heckling and taunting drew no reaction from the quiet stranger in the black hat.

Frustrated in their ignored efforts for some type of recognition, and tired of following the stranger and his canine companion, the street gang broke formation and planned their ambush. Two or three of the gang members ran ahead of the quiet stranger in the black hat and Murphy and stood in front of them to block their path. Other gang members formed a circle around the stranger and his dog. The entire gang laughed and heckled as the lead thugs stopped the progress of the quiet stranger and his faithful companion. The leader of the gang walked proudly to the front of the pack as the quiet stranger and Murphy stopped and stared at the group, now blocking their way.

"Well, now, it seems as if you have come to the end of the road, huh? You should have thought a little more carefully about walking around here in our neighborhood with fancy hats, fancy boots and nice clothes, and I am sure that you have a stack of money tucked away in a pocket of that fancy vest somewhere too."

Murphy looked up at his companion; his hair stood up, and the dog growled as the group backed off from the sight of the visibly angered dog. The quiet stranger in the black hat waved his arm in the air, and motioned for Murphy to calm down and to sit, and the dog immediately obeyed. The stranger quietly explained, "No, Murphy. This is part of the mission. We need to spread some light in their world."

"Whoa, spread some light, huh? Oh, wow! We are all so scared. Ya got you a big tough doggie too! You are a big guy! Damn, straight might be the biggest guy, I've evah seen! But you seem to be a pussy." The leader of the gang taunted them.

The quiet stranger in the black hat tilted his hat down; he pulled it down over his face, so you could only see his mouth and a few of his facial features under the wide brim of the hat. He stared at the group and the intense stare of his dark piercing eyes went right through every member of the gang. Collectively, the entire group took one-step backwards, and then they froze in place. The quiet stranger took one-step forward and then he stopped.

An ominous presence filled the air, and each member of the group felt a cold shiver go through their bodies. It was as if the air had suddenly changed from a summer climate to a midwinter climate in one brief second. Yet, despite the strange feelings and the overwhelming presence of the stranger, the leader of the gang had to display his misguided tenacity, and he continued to feel as if he could freely spout off.

He shook off the cold and the feelings of uneasiness.

A leader of a street thug gang always hides behind his numbers. That is where he feels that his strength is, in the people that he has convinced that he is judge, jury, and the false idol of, and this thug was no exception.

He pushed his way out of the crowd of his gang and smiled, while he smugly asked the quiet stranger in the black hat, "Why, are you here? You look lost, like you stepped out of time. Where ya going, dressed all fancy-like? You need to understand that you do not belong here and strangers passing through my neighborhood need to pay a price. Money is part of it and I am sure you have lots of it in one of your pockets, but that is only part of it. The other problem is that you did not ask if you could come through our territory. For that, you need to pay the price."

There was no response from the quiet stranger, only the continual dark stares from his black eyes.

The leader remained undaunted, and he continued to explain his plan, "Don't care who or what ya are, ya in our world now and that ain't good for you. And you really think that we are afraid of you, and your dog? There are fifteen of us, and one of you and an old dog. Shit, bein' honest, you is a really big guy, but since they call me Rage, cuz that is what I have inside of me all the time, I got to tell ya that we plan to cut ya big ass up into little pieces. Since I like dogs, your dog, we will let go, unless he attacks. If he attacks, we will carve him up too."

Rage reached into his pocket and took out a switchblade knife. With a smirk, he held the knife in the air and pressed the button to snap the blade into place while explaining, "Tellin' ya here and now that no one will ever find the pieces of you and they. . .."

The quiet stranger in the black hat finally spoke. He interrupted the leader in mid-speech, as he spoke in a low voice while asking the leader, "Do you really think that fifteen of your gang and a simple knife or two are enough? I have to ask you, do you really think that if you had five-thousand gang members and the same number of knives to help you, do you think that it would be enough? It will not be enough. I can assure you that it will not be enough."

When the stranger finished speaking, the blade of the knife, which Rage held in his hands, folded over, as if some unseen hand or force acted upon it. It seemed as if the blade of the knife melted in his hands. Shocked by the actions of the blade, Rage gave out a loud cry of surprise, and when the knife grew warmer and then burning hot in his hand, Rage tossed it away, and grabbed his hand in pain. The knife spun in the air, where it flashed and disappeared in a blinding light.

Most of the gang members turned and ran away while some of them fell to their knees in fear as to what they just witnessed. Rage, too; fell upon his knees on the sidewalk and he held his hands out in fear. He cried out as terror filled his soul, and curious bystanders surrounded the strange scene. Cars on the busy street stopped, and drivers and passengers stared out their windows at the mob scene, while horns blared and onlookers tried to catch a glimpse of what was happening on the city sidewalk.

While most of his gang fled in terror, Rage cried out, "What the hell! What the hell! Who the hell are you?"

As the quiet stranger leaned over and then bent down next to the leader of the gang, he tipped his hat, smiled and whispered, "Now, it seems as if you are not quite as brave as you thought that you were. I am who, or what, you could never imagine that I am. I recommend reading the book of Isaiah, in and around chapter thirty-seven, verse thirty-six. Now, Rage, or is it actually, Lionel? I suggest that you change your ways today, Mr. Lionel Jackson, because I will return someday to meet with you. I also suggest a new nickname. No more rage. You have my assurance that the change will be more than worthwhile."

The quiet stranger patted the terrified man on his back, jumped to his feet, and waved to his canine companion.

Murphy returned to a quick trot, and the faithful dog followed the quiet stranger. The two of them left the stunned gang members and amazed onlookers far behind, too stunned to move, all of them watching until they could no longer hear the click of the stranger's boots upon the sidewalk, and they disappeared from their view.

Within a short time and a few more city blocks, the two of them found themselves standing outside of the maze of residential high-rise buildings of the city projects. Specifically, they stood in front of the building, where on the sixteenth floor, next to a bedroom window in a cramped, dingy apartment; Calvin Wilson was listening to the last few innings of a baseball game. The quiet stranger in the black hat stood in the midsummer sun as it baked the sidewalk, with Murphy patiently standing next to him. The stranger looked up into the sky in the direction of the sixteenth-floor window. He spun around a few more times, as if to confirm his location and surroundings. With a wave of his hand, he indicated for Murphy to follow him, and they bounded up the long front steps to the apartment. The two visitors entered through the lobby and because of the precarious and vicious nature of the neighborhood; there was a set of locked doors, which required security badges to activate the various locks. Security badges, which the apartment building's residents possessed, but the quiet stranger in the black hat does not require or use security badges. He had a different type of pass assigned to him.

As he and Murphy approached the locked doors, the quiet stranger tipped the brim of his hat with his hand and seemingly, in response to his simple gesture, each door lock snapped open and in succession, the doors unlocked one-by-one, while the two of them passed by and entered the lobby. The quiet stranger in the black hat pointed to the door leading to the staircase, and the two of them, rapidly and effortlessly, climbed the many flights of stairs. Together, they reached the sixteenth floor of the building and they stood together in the hallway, right outside of apartment 16H.

Murphy sat and looked at his friend. The dog tilted his head as the quiet stranger in the black hat looked down and smiled at his canine companion. Since the dog's brilliant mind remained tuned into what was coming next, Murphy whimpered a little, because he knew the time had come for his next mission and for him to part ways with his beloved, quiet, and dark friend. The quiet stranger knelt down next to Murphy, and the two of them embraced for quite a while and held onto each other.

Finally, the quiet stranger spoke, "I know you miss Mr. Murphy and that you will miss me too. However, it is time now for your next mission, my dear friend. That door, which is right in front of us. He is very lonely, he cannot see, and he has trouble walking. Guide him, protect him and most of all, Murphy, you must love him as only a dog can love. Unconditionally, without rules and demands, without jealousy or prejudice."

Murphy the dog sat and held his paw out in front of him for the quiet stranger to grasp it, in order to show that he understood. The quiet stranger in the black hat reached into his vest pockets. He pulled out a collar with a brass dog tag hung upon it, and he gently reached over and placed the collar around Murphy's neck.

"This will tell his mother your name, and once she arrives home, she will be able to tell her son. Murphy, this will be your last mission here. Your next one will be filled with rainbows and filled with joy, when it finally comes time for you to rest, my dear friend. There, in a spectacular place, you will meet Mr. Murphy again. We will meet there too. Now, go."

Murphy jumped to his feet. He ran to the door of Calvin Wilson's apartment and immediately started to whimper and use his paws to dig and scratch at the base of the door. Inside the apartment in the bedroom, Calvin had just reached over to change the tuning dial from the baseball game to some music stations when he thought that he heard a noise at the front door. Randomly opening doors when you are blind and disabled, in this particular apartment house could cause some serious complications, and Calvin's mother warned him many times about such practices. The noises, at first, startled Calvin. Therefore, he listened very carefully for a long time, turning down the volume control on the radio and shuffling closer to the main hallway of the apartment, to listen clearly and carefully.

Calvin spoke aloud as he mumbled, "Why, it sounds as if it is a dog. Is it a dog out there? He shuffled slowly along a bit more, and carefully made his way over to the front door, feeling his way along the familiar route and holding his hands upon the walls to steady him and guide him too.

Standing by the door, Calvin asked in just a whisper, "Who is out there? Is there someone there? I hear a dog." Murphy tilted his ears, dug in with his paws harder, and he gave a gentle bark for a signal. "It is a dog! How strange! I love dogs."

Calvin lost all his apprehension and his fear that this could potentially be some type of set-up to fool Calvin into opening the door. Without any further hesitation, Calvin flipped the many locks on the door, and opened it widely. Immediately, Murphy the dog greeted him and the two newfound friends completed the connection, as only a dog could do.

Calvin started laughing as Murphy began loving his new friend and Calvin shouted out in joy, "A dog! And you are strong, friendly, and your fur is so soft! Hello, strange doggie, I wonder what this is all about and where you could have come from?"

As Calvin knelt down to greet Murphy the dog, Murphy looked over into the hallway and he barked three times at the quiet stranger in the black hat who smiled back, nodded, tipped his hat, and in one quick motion, he opened the staircase door and he disappeared.

"Hello? Did someone just go down the stairs? Hello?"

In the main lobby of the apartment hallway, the quiet stranger in the black hat stood in front of rows upon rows of mailboxes for the various apartments. He quickly scanned them and studied them until his eyes settled upon the box for apartment 16H. He reached inside of his vest pocket and removed a small package from the pocket . . . a package that contained a small music player. A special player with large buttons to allow for easier operation by disabled and blind persons. He gently pushed the package into the opening for 16H. He listened as he heard the package tumble and settle down into the box, and then he turned and walked out the front door of the apartment. Calvin's mother was slowly climbing the stairs to the apartment; she was weary from the heat and from a long day at work at the dry-cleaning store. While she held onto the iron railing, she could not help but notice the handsome stranger dressed all in black as he passed by her on the stairs. He stopped for a second, smiled at her, and tipped his hat. She smiled back and watched as he disappeared into the maze of the city. A warm and comforting feeling extended over her as she caught the stare of the quiet stranger in the black hat. She strangely and suddenly felt as if despite the weariness of her soul that from here on in, life would be better for her and Calvin. Why she felt that way, she did not know, but it was an immediate feeling that overcame her soul.

She commented in a quiet mumble, "How strange. I felt so exhausted just a second ago, and now, I feel a little refreshed and optimistic. Strange." She stared a little longer in order to try to catch a glimpse of the large man who just brushed by her so quickly upon the stairs, but he was already lost in the sidewalk bedlam of the city.

Once again, she mumbled as she made her way to the door of the apartment, "Wow! What a good-looking man. He looks wealthy, kinda strange for hanging around here. Seems as if he came out of nowhere."

Murphy

Conclusion

The Light of the World Gospel Church

About two years or so later, on a busy city street, not very far from the front door of the city projects where on the sixteenth-floor Calvin Wilson lived with Murphy the dog, a dingy old storefront now supported a new hand-painted sign over the top of the door frame. A young man, who the mean streets formerly knew by his nickname of "Rage," stood on a ladder in front of the storefront while he completed the installation of the sign. Another man stood at the base of the ladder, holding the legs in order to steady the structure.

On a dark blue background, the white letters stood out as they proudly displayed "The Light of the World Gospel Church" for the faithful and the unfaithful of the city to see.

"Looks good, Pastor Jackson. Really good for a can of paint and a brush. Someday, we will get us a real church, but for now, we gotta start somewhere."

"I think so. Not too bad," Pastor Jackson answered his friend.

"I will put the ladder back, inside," the helper said, as Pastor Jackson nodded and patted his friend on the back, while thanking him for his assistance.

The pastor stood and admired the sign as his helper disappeared into the church. While he stood there, Pastor Jackson caught the sound of metal tips of boots striking the sidewalk. The noise echoing from behind him sparked an extremely powerful memory, and a smile appeared on the face of the pastor. Before he could even turn around to confirm the source of the noise, he knew that the quiet stranger in the black hat had returned. He turned around, and sure enough, there the immense man stood. Pastor Jackson smiled and reached out his hand for the quiet stranger to grasp. The quiet stranger in the black hat smiled and held Pastor Jackson's hand, and he shook it warmly. Immediately a great feeling of warmth overtook the pastor, and he felt great comfort. No feelings of intense cold or terror filled moments during this meeting. Not this time. This was a much different meeting.

"Well, hello, stranger. I knew that someday you would return. You did tell me that you would and I counted on it. Not bad work, huh? For a converted street thug, that is."

He pointed up at the sign as the quiet stranger nodded his head in agreement.

"I guess you already know all of this story that I am gonna tell ya, but hey, I kinda figured that I will tell you anyhow. Bought me a used Bible about an hour after you left and you scared the, well, you know how you put terror in our hearts. Looked up that verse that you suggested and it was then that I knew that it was time to lose the rage. In more ways—in all ways! I knew why you came to me. My heart changed. My soul restored and renewed. The light turned on that all of this is for a greater purpose."

He laughed as the quiet stranger remained silent, but the stranger continued to smile and intensely stare, while remaining partially hidden under the wide brim of his hat.

"Ya sure don't say much. Anyway, I don't need to know exactly who you are. We all could not believe it, but we all know what we saw. Rather, keep that one in my heart. In looking back, we took your advice and I think that we did make a wise decision that day. Especially me. Ya know something, there big guy? I have got me a young man named Calvin in my little congregation here. He has this, here, faithful, old, Seeing-Eye dog that looks very familiar. You do work in mysterious ways for sure, quiet stranger. Is that your mission, to work your mysterious ways into this ragged world?"

The quiet stranger in the black hat finally spoke in a low, melodious voice as he gently placed his hand upon the shoulder of Pastor Jackson.

"Perhaps, among many missions. Above all. . .."

The stranger stopped speaking, pointed up at the words of the newly installed sign, and then he explained, "My mission is much the same as your new mission is, my friend. It is up to both of us now, to chase away loneliness by shedding more light in this world, and making sure that there is love in the midst of the darkness. Unconditional love always provides light into this dark world. Love, without rules and demands, without selfishness, jealousy or prejudice. That is the true light of this world. Please, keep up the good work and continue to shine some light down upon all of this. I can assure you, just as I did on that fateful day of our first meeting, that in the end, it will be more than worthwhile."

The quiet stranger in the black hat smiled. He then tipped his hat, turned and walked briskly away. Pastor Jackson could not help but smile. The pastor had a strong feeling that he knew from where the dark stranger had come from, but he did not have any clue as to where he was off to now. He stood and watched as the quiet stranger in the black hat moved quickly along the sidewalks of the city. Pastor Jackson watched for a long time until he disappeared from his view and he could no longer hear the click of the metal tips of his boots upon the sidewalk.

THE END

When the Night Closes In

Part 1

A Lover's Tangled Web

In late August 2015, in the bedroom of an exclusive condominium unit located on the affluent side of the old city, a wild romp of lust between two clandestine lovers just concluded. Love, such as what they just shared, always seems so easy, so full of joy and excitement and the allure of the forbidden aspect of their relationship, only added to the passion and excitement. These two lovers might be deeply in love; however, it was difficult to tell. True love has no rules and seldom adheres to boundaries. It is often difficult to determine where morals collapse and true love begins.

When enveloped in the wild pangs of pleasure, these types of secret lovers only dream of their love for each other and nothing else. They live only for the moment, for their precious-few moments of uninhibited ecstasy and mutual pleasure. When passion captures the lover's hearts, there is very little concern if they are going to hurt anyone.

Those thoughts never cross their minds.

Then again, in the light of the day, it all seems so different and it seems so easy, but then it all becomes dark and desperate when the night closes in.

"Oh, give me another week or two with him. I need a few wild romps in the sack to boost his self-esteem and I will be able to convince him rather easily to accept your report. You know, the report that you spent such considerable time in researching and writing," Jennifer Tolland smugly said as she rolled over in the bed towards her lover.

"He is so easy to manipulate, and once I have him where I want him, then our plans will all come together."

Richie Stafford smiled and leaned over, while one at a time, kissing each one of Jennifer's exposed and bare breasts.

"I guess. Jennifer, I have to tell you that I hate the thought of sharing you with him. It turns my stomach."

Jennifer laughed, and she broke away from Richie's grasp as she rolled out the side of the bed and stood up. Richie's gaze ran up and down her gorgeous naked body and he admired her captivating beauty.

"Well, you need to get over that fact, Richie. After all, he is my husband and part of playing the role of a good solid and upstanding wife to Senator Tolland is to smile, attend functions, dress elegantly, tend to his house, and on occasion, humor him by allowing him to make love to me. All he cares about is work, anyhow. There is no passion involved in our love sessions. It is just a chore for me, similar to cooking or doing the laundry for him. You have no equal as a lover, my precious Richie."

Richie frowned as he rolled over in the bed; he folded his arms across his bare chest and fretted over the thoughts.

"I guess, Jennifer. Still, I have to say that it bothers the hell out of me." Jennifer grabbed her undergarments from a pile of clothes tossed on the floor in the previous throes of passion. And once she sorted them, she slowly dressed.

"Stay focused on the plan, my love. Soon, the world will be in shock and awe when they catch the good, kind and honest, Senator Tolland taking money from a wealthy group of real estate investors. While he wrangles in the middle of unexplainable and shocking corruption, we will be lost overseas, with new names, new identities and a new life together. We will make love every minute of every day."

She finished dressing and leaned over the bed to give Richie a quick kiss.

"I have to go. I will slip out the back door here. Right now, we need to be careful now that we are so close. I will send you some text messages later and sneak a call in when I can."

When she went to pull away and stand up, Richie grabbed her arm. He pulled her close, slapped her on the backside and asked, "So baby, ya like the diamond bracelet, or what? It is not too wide or huge on your wrist, is it?"

"No, it is perfect! Of course, I love it, Richie. It is gorgeous. Thank you so much. You are not only an amazing lover, but an amazing man too! Honestly, I wish you did not have the inscription on the back. You know how I do not want to leave any kind of trail at all, but it is lovely. I will wear it to the dinner engagement at the hotel tonight. Gordon and I have to attend this evening, and I hope to sneak away and call you when I can. In the meantime, I have to listen and pretend that I am interested in some boring ass discussion about who the hell cares, or even knows what they are talking about. I will wear a low-cut dress, allow a few old jerks to check out the top of my boobies, throw down a few strong martinis, get a little numb, shut my mouth and smile and nod for hours."

"Jennifer, please, have no concern. I needed to buy you something special in order to honor our love. No one could ever tell that the numbers, one-sixty-eight, and an etched tree drawing, would line up to the address of this unit. It is our little secret. Besides, Michanetti has the lease for this joint anyhow. No way, can it be tied to our love and us."

"I guess."

"What will you tell the good Senator Tolland about where you got it from, when he spots it on your wrist? It is not as if ya can't notice it?"

"Oh, shit! Do not even give that a second thought. No problem with that one. He will not remember. When we were first dating, and he had his hands inside my pants every day, he bought me all kinds of fabulous jewelry and lavish gifts. I will tell him it was a random gift that *he* gave to me years ago. . .."

When the Night Closes In

Part 2

Instincts Never Fail

New Jersey Senator Gordon Tolland had a solid reputation. Young, happily married to a gorgeous wife, no children yet, but in his mind, the future plans included some. Gordon was handsome, brilliant, and charismatic. He maintained a squeaky-clean image and after his first successful term as a freshman state senator; he won a unanimous reelection to office. Now, in his second term, the very wealthy and former attorney and assistant prosecutor, was a legend and folk hero among the general population for his honest, no-nonsense approach to legislation. He initially won election by telling the people that he would promise to stay out of the spotlight, and he promised not to take campaign money from any special interests and deal openly and honestly with all issues. The media did not take kindly to the good senator's intentions. After all, honest politicians are boring and mundane and do not bring riveting headlines and fill the advertising coffers. Controversial, shady politicians sell but boring good guys do not.

Perpetually, on the prowl and lurking in dark shadows, watching and waiting for that money shot, the ruthless press thought they had caught him one time in a compromising and difficult situation. Some photographers for hire, who follow people such as Senator Gordon

Tolland everywhere, snapped a picture of him kissing the cheek of, and with his arm around, a beautiful young woman outside of a local Irish Pub. The disappointment became profound when the woman proved to be Senator Tolland's youngest sister and the older woman laughing and watching the scene from afar, to be their mother.

His enemies were many; he was not popular amongst his peers for his independent third-party affiliation, his staunch stance on conservative issues in a primarily liberal political environment, and his intense desire to gather all the facts before making a judgment. The lobbyists gave chase when he first arrived in the state senate. They all quickly gave up when their efforts to lobby, wine and dine him, while promoting their individual agendas to him, all failed miserably. Now, they did not support him, and did their best to disparage his efforts. The corrupt operators in and around the state were not happy that they seemingly could not sway or motivate him with money, beautiful women, tickets to the baseball games, free meals at exclusive restaurants, and any other of the usual "incentives" that politicians usually jump for to make deals and pass special interest legislation.

On this waning afternoon, Senator Gordon Tolland sat behind his desk in his office. He picked up from his desk a booklet of research papers prepared for him to review on some pending legislation, and he carefully studied them once again. This research paper contained material in which he had read carefully many, many times before this afternoon. In fact, Senator Tolland had read it cover-to-cover more times than he wanted to admit. The papers pertained to some legislation that now was set for debate and a vote for the upcoming state senate sessions within the next few days. It was not the first time this legislation had made its way onto the senate floor. The first few rounds on this legislation, initiated angst-filled days of heated debate. He sat back in his chair, flipped the cover of the report, and started to read the information once again. He swore that it was at least the tenth time that he had read this same report. An independent consultant had prepared the report, and on the surface, the report seemed quite concise and thorough.

The not-for-profit environmental organization that his wife sat on the executive board of recommended the independent consultant to prepare the report. The organization then presented the same information to the special senate committee formed to study this matter. The author was a consultant that his wife and the board touted for being impartial, whose views were seemingly independent, and who was a leading expert on the environmental impact of real estate developments. The writer of the report was a man named Richard Stafford, a man whom Gordon had never met; however, when he checked into the suggestion by his wife's organization, he certainly had an outstanding resume. Gordon felt his wife's advice was solid, and the recommendation was a good one, because the report was so detailed and comprehensive. Yet, for some reason, Gordon remained unconvinced on the pending legislation. Legislation, which involved selling off large chunks of state-owned land to independent developers, in order to acquire badly needed funding for the state coffers. Funding required, for some hope of offsetting unpopular tax increases, and funding, which lessens the impact on the working people of the State of New Jersey, during very difficult economic times.

As Gordon studied the report, he had to admit how well written and extensively researched the subject matter appeared to be. Despite his admittance, Gordon felt as if there still were parts missing, something under the surface that was not readily apparent or had not yet come to light. While on the surface, the plan seemed to be an easy one to approve, and a clichéd, "no-brainer" for the senate to vote in favor of the massive sale and fundraiser, there was something that did not stick well with Gordon. Even though the debate had raged on for weeks as a prelude to the pending vote, Gordon felt as if it was all rushed. The report that he held in his hands advised that the state should immediately move to finalize a quick sale to prime real estate developers before the developers walked away to a competing piece of land in New York. For some nagging reason, the advice did not sit with him well enough to throw all of his support towards a quick sale.

There were too many what ifs? Gordon did not do well in acting fast on situations when there were lingering, what ifs. . ..

What if they held out for a while longer and hired a marketing agent to test the market? Perhaps they had not fully investigated the potential of federal funding approval for highway improvement, which could then lead the interstate through these parcels of land. What if that was the case? If that were true, then the value of these parcels would skyrocket with an interstate frontage or convenient access off the extension of the roads.

Gordon sat back in his chair and pondered the situation more, and then he once again thumbed through the report by the consultant and found the section on the potential interstate extension and expansion. He scoured the opinion of the report's author once again. In the report, the researcher clearly stated that even if the federal government approved the funding to extend the interstate, the topography of the land would bring the roads miles and miles away from these parcels. The cost of blasting away the mountains of rock that was in the path to these parcels would make the construction of the beneficial route very expensive, and for those reasons, the report discounted the possibility of the building of any highways or major roads close to these parcels. The mountains, combined with the hilly terrain, would force engineers to plot a lower cost route. Gordon even read opinions by a professional civil engineer stating that would be the case.

There it was, plain as a day in the report, many opinions of experts. Gordon Tolland was not an expert in road construction and civil engineering practices, so what was his apprehension? On the other hand, maybe the old real estate adage of location, location, location, was not what was bothering Gordon so deeply and profoundly. Perhaps his apprehension was over the use of the word "immediately" when recommending the sale; sooner rather than later. Yes, in his heart Gordon felt as if there was another reason, a far deeper reason, as to why this all felt so rushed along. Who were these investors from an unknown corporation who, for some reason, desired this land so hastily and so badly? What did they see that the author of this report and the state committee did not? Gordon was an instinct guy; he went with his initial reactions and it served him well. It served him right now, in his new career in public office, as it did when he was a trial attorney. He did not plan to change his ways now.

There was a hard knock at the door to his office, and before he could answer or move from behind his desk, the door swung open. Gordon looked up and smiled, as he saw his longtime partner in the county prosecutor's office and friend, Charles "Chuck" McCracken, walk into his office. Gordon knew that it was Chuck at his door, even before he saw him, because he did not have the courtesy to wait for Gordon to answer his knock before he walked into the office.

Chuck did not play by too many rules and if you looked up the definition of "Hard-boiled" in the dictionary, it might just have a picture of Chuck McCracken aligned with it.

Sure, he was older now, his hair was all grey, he walked a little bent over, drank too much Scotch, but his chiseled good looks still remained, and despite the fashion and current styles, Chuck still wore his same old flattop haircut.

Gordon Tolland also knew that in this world, there was no better friend than Charles "Chuck" McCracken was.

"Hey, Gordy. What the hell is goin' on these days? Ya studyin' sumthin'. Ya got that look on ya puss. Got an idea of what it is too. So, any decision on the Land-Gate bullshit sale?"

"You know me too well. No, no, not yet, Chuck. Still, mulling over the research. In fact, I was just reading this consultant's report again."

"Still, reading that bullshit?"

"Yes, still."

Chuck pulled out a guest chair and sat in front of the desk of his friend. Charles McCracken was now retired for about three months from the prosecutor's office, and he had extra time on his hands. Extra time for Chuck McCracken was always trouble because he was a high-energy guy. Gordon always wondered if he would stay retired for very long. Chuck and Gordon were partners in the prosecutor's office until Gordon decided to enter politics. Charles had been the partner of Gordon's father, in that same office until the early and sudden death of Gordon's father. When Chuck heard that his deceased partner's son had graduated from law school with honors and passed the state bar exam with a remarkably high score, then Chuck lobbied for his old partner's son to receive strong consideration for an appointment to the prosecutor's office in the county.

A New Jersey county, known to be a hotbed of crime.

Crime of an organized nature.

It proved to be a wise and worthy choice for the county officials to have made because they made an exceptional team and won many cases. In fact, no one could actually recall any case that the team of McCracken and Tolland Junior ever lost.

Despite an age difference of thirty or so years, they were very close friends, and since Gordon's father passed away,

Chuck stepped in to be a father figure in Gordon Tolland's life. Chuck now passed his retirement time by driving his wife crazy and being some type of unofficial consultant to Gordon. Charles never minced words, especially when he was speaking in confidence to his former partner. Chuck McCracken saw his role now as some type of unofficial advisor to the senator, or being a sounding board, but he was very comfortable speaking his opinion to Gordon. Charles "Chuck" McCracken willingly provided his opinion, even if the senator did not ask for it or if he chose to follow it.

In fact, Chuck McCracken had no qualms about sharing his opinions with anyone.

"Gordy, the way that I see it is that if you do not move on this, then you are screwed. If you wait much longer, then the fallout will be horrific. Senator Buckwald is pushing hard for this and he has made it a pet project to keep you in his gun sights. You're the independent vote they all need. If it goes by party lines, then your vote could decide it all. The media loves to stomp all over you. Buckwald for some reason, leads the charge too. Therefore, it becomes darker by the second and the night closes in around you, my friend. What is the hold up and apprehension? Taxpayers are screaming for relief and this land can fetch a huge amount of money. Not that the money will mean jackshit anyhow, it will help, but it will be just another drop in the bucket until youse guys eventually raise taxes. If you vote no, then you are not going to be a hero in the senate, or with the media, and the voters will piss all over you. Just to make it even worse, this is a reelection year. The media will have your handsome puss plastered all over the news broadcasts, and you will need to join me in retirement. Then we can sit around together, suck down Scotch, pick our asses and twiddle our thumbs."

Gordon nodded, smirked a bit, while waving his hand in

the air as he said, "I am not concerned about being popular, Chuck. You know that. We were not popular in the past and I do not expect that to change very much if at all."

"Good for you, Gordy. Always remember what I told ya years ago, if you are everyone's best friend, then you never stood for anything. So, all of this coming down on top of you and the reelection pressure, you know, da bullshit, but ya need to shake ya ass and make a decision."

Gordon reacted to Chuck's statement with a frown. He stared at his friend, shifted uneasily in his chair and told Chuck, "I know all of that and I appreciate your honesty. I just feel there is something that we missed here." Gordon picked up the report from his desk, waved it in the air, and continued, "Do not get me wrong. This report is comprehensive and appears on the surface to be sound advice, but I have a gut feeling to wait, market the land with some real estate marketing pros and perhaps, the land can be sold for even more money."

"Gut feeling, huh? What else ya got goin' on?"

"This corporation that wants to purchase the land and develop it. The Marckpan Corporation. Some type of strange corporation formed to look around America and buy up land to preserve natural areas forever more. What kind of business is that? Who puts up that much money to save trees and lakes and trout? Never heard of them. Other than some land deals out, in of all places," Gordon rolled his eyes a bit, "in Wyoming . . . they have not brokered any significant deals. The executive board is a bunch of no names. People who seem to be very wealthy, but at what they did, in order to achieve wealth, is somewhat vague. I see investors in stocks, owners of a large group of plastic factories, some type of family business with recycled auto parts, which turned into a retail empire. I never heard of any of them before this and any research on it is a dead end. It makes me very uncomfortable. Other than environmental concerns, what do these no names see in a massive parcel of land in New Jersey that we do not? What real estate backgrounds do they all have that we do not have access to?"

Chuck put his feet up on his friend's desk, tilted back in the chair and placed his hands behind his head. He rubbed his hands furiously across the top of his buzzed, cut head. Gordon knew that habit. His friend now agreed with his apprehension.

Chuck was deep in thought until he asked, "Wyoming, huh? Now, they are out-of-state folks, who suddenly and miraculously show up in New Jersey with loads of dough to save trees. Screw the trees and trout. The key is the parcels that they say they will develop. That's where the dough is. Did they tell youse guys what areas of the parcels they would build upon?"

Gordon shook his head to indicate no.

"Ya sure the interstate ain't coming close to this someday."

"The report says it will not. Too costly to route it that way. Only one engineer's opinion though."

"Gotcha, Gordy. I see, and now ya got my radar up too. Smells rather organized to me. New Jersey, land of trout streams, pollution, and organized crime. Maybe a front for something. Ya think it is overseas dough backing 'em? Ain't there some kind of federal laws 'bout selling state lands to foreigners? And if it is not overseas assholes, then if you know what I mean by organized, I mean as in mob organized."

"I just do not know, Chuck, and yes, there might be obscure laws about land sales to foreign investors. There are laws about everything these days, but it takes time to investigate them. That is my point! All this rushing because these investors waved a huge sum of money in the air and set a deadline or they will pull the offer. I need more time to connect some dots. On the surface, it is innocent. Wealthy investors looking to preserve the environment, save trees, preserve pristine lakes and streams for natural reasons and develop some small parcels of land to recoup their investment costs. All out of the goodness of their heart to save the world. I do not buy it. Then again, I do not know. Time is one thing that I do not have. The vote will be in a few days."

"Yup. Ya got that right. The flames are licking your ass now and the night is closing in. Your wife's organization turned you on to this report writing guy, huh?" Chuck said while he rubbed his chin, and then waved his hand across the top of his buzz cut again. He knew Gordon's gut instincts from the courtroom and he grew to pay attention to them and not discount them.

"Yes, and he has a solid reputation in environmental circles as well as real estate, but this appears to have been the only significant paper of this type that he ever wrote, but that is not the issue. It is deeper than that."

"Whatcha mean?"

"It is too well written, Chuck. As in polished by a pro, written."

"Gotcha. Like a ringer wrote it. Could be innocent. Maybe the guy knows his shit, has good ideas, but cannot convey them, so he hires a ghostwriter to write it all fancy for him."

"Yes. That could be true."

"Say, Gordy, why did your wife's organization recommend him for the independent study?"

"Because of the environmental concerns and the Marckpan Corporation's supposed interest and pledge for natural preservation of portions of land deals. Part of the deal is to preserve wildlife areas in natural states and leave some glorious trout streams unaltered and protected on the parcels. Despite what most people see from the New Jersey Turnpike, we have some wonderful trout streams and amazing natural areas here."

Chuck frowned and studied Gordon for a few minutes.

It was readily apparent that trout streams and natural areas were not high on Chuck's interest or concern list.

The grizzled attorney reinforced that fact with a continued frown and a mumble of, "Yeah, well, whatever. The only fishin' I want to do is for my Scotch bottle in the back of the cupboard and on my wife's gorgeous naked body."

Gordon held back a comment at his friend's lack of concern for trout streams and frank comments on his married life, and continued to explain, "They are advocating for the sale as an organization in the interest of helping with tax relief, combined with environmental preservation, and what they claim to be, the minor development of parcels. It is a lobby movement on their behalf. Jennifer agrees that some lands should be developed, but she volunteers for the executive board, because she is such a staunch advocate for environmental protection causes."

"Makes sense, Gordy. I think. Let me ask ya, what the hell would New Jersey do with all of this so-called natural land, if ya don't sell it? Turn it into some kinda designated state forest or some bullshit like that? More land to maintain without funds. The state needs money right now. We are in a fiscal crisis. Right?"

"Well, yes, Chuck. You are correct. Right now, the state considers it surplus land. It is a protected state land and yes, official, state forests require maintenance."

"What is it called now?"

"A state-owned, protected wildlife management area and naturally preserved area. No formal maintenance, no budget line items, many volunteers working to keep the land clean. Basically, public land for natural recreational use."

"What a bunch of bullshit that is. Gordy, who comes up with this nonsense?"

"I am not sure. Some people love the land. I know it is

not your bag . . . but anyway, I guess that designation saves the maintenance funds. Say, I know that look, Chuck. You and I brainstormed too much over the years. What is bugging you?"

"Ah, your wife? Does she know him?"

"Know who?"

"This writer of the report."

"I do not think so. Well, perhaps, at a meeting or two in past business. I am only guessing. Why do you ask?"

"Don't know. Not exactly. You are not the only one who goes by your gut, Gordy. Why not hire your own engineer and consultant for a second lookie?"

"Chuck, I would love to. I would even pay for it out of my own money, but there is no time left. This deal all came about so quickly. Too many deadlines and what ifs."

Gordon looked at his friend and shook his head. His mysterious and suspicious nature and behavior were so familiar to him. Gordon was uncomfortable with the look on his friend's face and the question about his wife's relationship with the author of the report; therefore, he decided to change the subject.

"Are you attending the dinner tonight with your wife? How is Michelle? I bet she is sick of you hanging around the house!"

"She just told me that! In fact, she pushed me over here to hang out with you because she said I was being a pain in her gorgeous ass today. Other than me getting on her nerves, she is well. I need to find a little pastime. Maybe throw my hat in the ring for attorney general or something like that. Anyhoo . . . 'bout tonight. No, Michelle has other plans. She gets bored stiff with all that elbow rubbing. Same old, Michelle. Great lady, a beautiful lady with a great ass, a heart of gold, and a woman, who has zero tolerance for horn blowing bullshit. Gordy, you know the drill and my wife does too. However, yes, I do plan to be there. After all, I got to watch over you."

When the Night Closes In

Part 3

He is Always Watching

In a far corner of the parking lot in the rear of the condominium complex located at 168 Birch Road, Mr. Richard Stafford walked over to the driver's door of an expensive sports car. He looked around as if he was somewhat nervous, reached into his pocket for the car keys, placed them in the door lock, spun the lock, and climbed into the driver's seat of the vehicle. The engine started, Richard put the car in gear, and he sped off. What Mr. Stafford did not realize was that when he reached into his pocket to pull out his car keys, he accidentally dropped a sales receipt.

It fluttered into the air and settled upon the asphalt of the parking lot.

There it sat, for just a moment or two, until a highly polished, black boot pressed down upon the paper to prevent it from blowing away. An immense man, larger than the word large can describe, wearing a wide-brimmed, black hat, reached down, moved his boot and picked up the receipt. He glanced at it, placed it in the pocket of the black vest that he was wearing, turned, and walked briskly away.

"So, your little honey has her old man in her back pocket. You are sleeping with her. She is still sleeping with her husband, guiding him around by both of his heads. That jackass, Buckwald is in our pocket too. Geez, this is ugly now. This sure is a gettin' to be a damn mess, Richie. You expect to pull this off, and all you want is a cool mill, and you and the former Mrs. Senator, run away somewhere, huh?"

"That is, it, Tony. She can't stay married to a convicted felon. It is a done deal. Mr. Clean will vote in favor of the land sale, your phony company can buy the land; you can do what you want with it, or sell it back to someone down the road for triple your profit. The law nabs Mr. Clean with his hand in the cookie jar, takin' the payoffs that we plant in his checking account, and most of all, he is finally out of your way. The land is just a bonus in the deal."

Tony Michanetti smiled and rubbed his forehead as he leaned back in the chair. He told Richie, "I like it. Tolland is a major pain in the ass. Besides, I have some insiders in Washington, D.C. who tell me that there are rumblings about federal grants for highway extensions in that area. You know, traffic congestion studies, or some horseshit like that. If the roads go through or even come close to this land, I can tear the shit out of that land and develop retail, residential, commercial, man oh man, the dough rolling in would be remarkable."

"I covered that in the report too, with some nonsense. Paid off an alcoholic civil engineer to write some bullshit about rock blasting as a smokescreen for the route of the interstate. Bunch of technical stuff."

"An alcoholic engineer, huh? Where do you find these losers? Whatever, but okay, I like that, Richie. But what if they hire an alternate study or retain their own engineer? And there ain't no drunk bum involved?"

"Nobody smart enuff to do that, and no time left to do it. Besides, once Mr. Clean has some more tastes of paradise, he will vote for anything. She is amazing in bed."

Tony picked up a pen from his desk and nervously tapped it on the desk's surface as he drifted deeper into thought.

"Screw the wildlife reserves and preserved trout streams on the parcels that the phony corporation will agree to preserve, in order to nail the vote on the sale. With Tolland, out of the way, I can pay everyone else off. The trout streams have a road frontage. No way am I passing that up. We will fill them in, dam 'em up and carve that land up like the surface of the moon. They can all stick their fly rods up their asses. A highway going through there will make that land worth a fortune."

Tony reached over the desk and shook hands with Richard. Both men smiled as Tony reached into his desk and pulled out two cigars and an envelope.

"Here ya go, Richie. Here are the checks to deposit in his account. In addition, here are a few celebration cigars. They are Cuban

Lisa Mackworth was a small-time hood, and she was not too proud of it either. Actually, she was a drug addict and specifically a heroin addict. This terrible drug habit that she developed a few years back, forced her into a life of small-time crime, some occasional prostitution, which roughly consisted of some conning of wealthy, older men with giant bellies and terrible breath, out of quite a bit of money to spend an adventurous evening with a pretty woman.

All the usual stuff that goes on within the cruel and often unseen world.

Lisa was still very attractive, slim and trim, a nice figure. She could smile and melt some hearts, then achieve her goals and buy another fix. It tore her up, but she just could not find her way out of the mess that she was in these days.

Comparatively, this gig seemed easy. First, a fancy hairdo with some front money, then she put on some extra make-up, she had to wear this expensive and stunning dress that they gave her, walk into a bank, deposit some checks with the deposit slips they gave her and collect a nice little sum of money.

In comparison to enduring horrible sex with big bellied, ugly men with non-working parts and pieces and terrible breath—this one was a relative piece of cake.

The typewritten note that she had in her hands, with the step-by-step script, told her that if the teller asks, simply explain that you are the new assistant to Senator Tolland. That will work. But she never even heard of the guy, so Lisa hoped that the teller did not quiz her further on Senator Tolland. Oh well, the money was good, and she was lucky to have come across the deal. A friend of a friend, just another one of the countless street thugs around, had managed the deal. She did feel bad about how this was an obvious set-up of some big shot politician, because deep down, in a former life, she cared. However, right now, she required some chemicals to run through her veins, therefore, she did not ask questions, she just needed the money.

"Are you new to Senator Tolland's staff?" The teller asked Lisa as she processed the deposits.

At first, Lisa fumbled the answer a bit, then she brushed it off as nervousness at the new position, "Oh, oh, oh, yes, I am. I hope I do a good job."

The teller smiled, handed back the receipts for the deposit and told Lisa, "You will. Good luck with the new job. He is a wonderful man. Very handsome too!"

Lisa joked her way through it from there, "Well, yes he is, but that is a bonus of the new position that I cannot comment on, if you know what I mean! Thank you. See you, soon."

"Good evening, Senator Tolland, Mrs. Tolland. I think you know my wife, Ann Buckwald."

"Yes, good evening, Senator Buckwald. Mrs. Buckwald, it is nice to see you again. You might also remember my wife, Jennifer."

"Of course, how could you ever forget such a lovely lady," Senator Buckwald shook hands with Gordon, and then gently took Mrs. Tolland's right hand, kissed it and winked at her.

Oh shit, what a jackass, Jennifer Tolland thought to herself. Right in front of his wife, he behaves like that. He acts like that even after today when Richie dropped him off the pay-off money from Tony.

Gordon turned to Chuck McCracken, who was standing next to the group. The old attorney was slowly sipping a double Scotch, poured neat, while peering over the rim of the glass.

"I think you may have also met in years past, my old partner from our prosecutor days, and now, my close friend and advisor, Mr. Charles McCracken."

"Yes, Charles. How have you been? The county prosecutor's office misses you. You were the best."

"Oh yeah, they miss me, huh? I am fine. Call me, Chuck, there, Senator Huff n' Puff. I will give ya a warning. Other than Gordy here, I don't usually trust folks who use my full and proper name."

Senator Buckwald bristled a bit at the gruff comments of the old prosecutor.

Chuck continued between sips, "I am retired, but doin' fine. Thanks, I always did my best." Chuck then lifted his eyes over the rim of the drink glass. He took a sip and stared directly at Senator Buckwald's eyes while saying, "Have to tell ya, that I can't stand crooks, connivers, chiselers, and thieves. As of late, I am itchin' to get back in the game, ya know, track a few more bad guys down."

The implications of his statement and the subject of his stare were somewhat less than obscure.

Chuck mumbled a little more about getting back in the game, while staring around the room, then checking out, and admiring the low-cut dress that the senator's wife was wearing. He took another sip of his Scotch, pointed one finger in the direction of Mrs. Buckwald, and smiled.

Chuck then commented, "Better not move too fast there, Mrs. Buckwald, or that mighty chest of yours might escape from that dress and take out ya eyes."

Mrs. Buckwald smiled at Chuck's coy remark, but Senator Buckwald's eyes burned. First the comment about cooks, connivers, chiselers, and thieves, and then his lewd remark about his wife's chest. Clearly, Charles "Chuck "McCracken was not the senator's favorite person, and there remained no doubt that the feelings were mutual.

Chuck McCracken was one of a kind.

Once Chuck made his splash, more greetings extended amongst the group, and some small talk ensued, when Mrs. Buckwald commented on the lovely diamond bracelet that Mrs. Tolland wore for this evening's gala event.

"Oh yes, Gordon gave it to me many years ago, when we first met. I recently found it buried in the back of my jewelry box and thought it would be perfect for tonight."

"I gave that to you? I must have settled a good case, Jenny!" Gordon commented and stared at the amazing diamond bracelet gracing his wife's wrist.

"Why, yes, of course . . . you gave it to me, it was in the first year of our dating. Do you remember that wonderful week that we spent in San Francisco, at the country club on the bay? How could you forget that week? Sometimes, Gordy, your memory, you have too much on your mind these days, my love." Jennifer Tolland reached up and lovingly gave her husband a kiss on the cheek.

The entire group laughed at the thought that Gordon

could forget giving such an expensive gift. Well, almost all the group laughed.

Chuck McCracken continued to peer over his glass, sip his Scotch and observe.

Chuck did not laugh.

Instead, he thought how that kiss was a phony and staged to deflect attention from the fact that Gordy did not recognize the bracelet. Chuck knew his best friend too well; in his mind, he thought how Gordy did not usually forget things. Nothing.

"Might I be able to see it closer? It is gorgeous. You are so lucky to have a man with such remarkable taste, Jennifer," Mrs. Buckwald asked as Jennifer reached out to display the bracelet and show Ann Buckwald. When Jennifer reached out, the latch suddenly gave way, and the bracelet tumbled onto the carpet of the ballroom.

The bracelet landed at the feet of Chuck McCracken.

"Oh no! I must have not latched the bracelet tightly enough. I hope that it is not damaged!" Jennifer exclaimed in concern at the sight of the bracelet tumbling upon the carpet. Chuck bent down, scooped it up from the carpet rather quickly, and he held it in his hands.

He closely examined it and commented, "No, it is fine. It landed softly. The carpet here softened the blow of the fall. If it fell on the dance floor, it might have been a different story."

While Chuck held the bracelet and studied the jewelry for potential damage, he could not help but notice the inscription on the back. Some numbers; one-sixty-eight, which he recorded in his mind, along with a small drawing of a tree that he noticed inscribed next to the numbers. How unusual, he thought as he handed the bracelet to Gordon. In his still sharp and inquisitive mind, honed from years of attorney interrogations, investigations, grilling, and questioning of people providing testimonies, more than just a few skeptical thoughts now arose.

Innocent until proven guilty was not exactly how Chuck McCracken operated. He tended to turn the two words around in their order.

Chuck's eyes quickly darted over to Mrs. Tolland's eyes. The amount of concern in her eyes, while she studied Chuck's careful observation of the inscription, only helped to reinforce Chuck's natural suspicions. She looked away when she felt Chuck's eyes studying her, but her concern forced her eyes to return to the bracelet and the situation. Now Chuck was on full alert. He made a very good living for many years by reading people's eyes.

"Here, Gordy, it is fine. No harm. Put it back on your wife's wrist and latch it tight. Too expensive a piece to have it falling all over the place. I am going outside to enjoy a cancer stick."

Chuck handed the bracelet to his friend, reached into his suit jacket pocket for his smokes, took his drink glass and headed for the outside smoking area.

As he slowly walked away, he heard the banter of political wrangling begin.

"Say there, Senator Tolland, I hate to talk business at a charity fundraiser, but about the Land-Gate deal. Our taxpayers are looking for relief, and they convey happiness over tax cuts with their votes. I cannot imagine what your apprehension is on this deal, Gordy. It is an environmental win-win, a ton of extra millions for the coffers, great headlines for all of us, profound statements in the press for our concern for taxpayers, a piece of land that the state will never use in a million years."

Chuck McCracken stopped a server while he scurried across the ballroom floor, and Chuck told the server in his low and gruff voice, "This event sucks big time, a bunch of boring ass, self-fulfilling jack-offs and big blowhards. Where can I smoke?"

The server smiled, laughed, and pointed to a wide set of double doors located at the far end of a hallway, next to the ballroom.

"Over there. Out on the balcony. I agree about the blowhards too. Politicians, of course," the server commented.

Chuck smiled and said, "Here pal, this is now empty."

Chuck tilted the glass back and swigged the rest of the drink.

"Can you bring me another double Scotch? Can you make it neat? I hate standing on line for drinks. Get me top-shelf stuff. Can't deal with headaches in the morning. I will be out on the balcony here with a smoke or two. Here is twenty bucks for your effort."

The server took the twenty-spot, tucked it in the top pocket of his shirt and told Chuck, "No sweat. Give me a minute or two."

Out on the balcony, surprisingly, the late summer air was crisp and cool. Chuck McCracken took a deep breath of the air and swallowed it in. Sometimes, air conditioning and its false delivery of cool air grows wearisome and the crispness of the night air is a welcome change. Autumn was on the heels of summer now, and there was a sense that the change of the seasons grew steadily closer as the night closed in.

"Here is your Scotch, sir," the server said as he handed the drink off to Chuck, who mumbled a thank you. Chuck took a sip of it as the server disappeared inside the facility. Chuck steadily sipped the drink for a few gulps; he needed the liquid magic to soften the harsh feelings growing within his soul. Feelings that he hoped for his old and faithful friend's sake were not true.

Chuck reached in his suit jacket, pulled out his pack of cigarettes, tapped one loose and stuck it in his mouth. Before he could reach for his cigarette lighter hidden deep within the maze of his suit, Chuck heard the distinctive "click" in the air of a lighter being struck. He turned to his side and in the night, he saw the flame ignite. The old attorney then realized that he was so deep in thought, and perhaps working through some angst, that he had not heard the approaching footsteps of the man who was now holding the lighter out towards him.

Chuck leaned into the flame, sucked deeply and spoke out of the side of his mouth, while lighting the smoke, "Thanks . . . pal . . . I appreciate that. Nice night, huh? Air is better out here, even sucking on these cancer sticks, then it is in there."

Chuck turned around to look closer at the man who had lit his cigarette and he was startled at the appearance of him. He almost gasped as he studied what had to be the largest man that he had ever seen, who now stood right next to him. The huge man snapped the lighter closed and placed it inside the pocket of a black vest that he was wearing. On second thought, Chuck's mind spun with the memory, because he recalled how he had seen a man just as large once before, a stranger who looked just the same as this man did.

It was a few years ago, now.

Chuck mumbled, "Damn. . .. Where did you come from?"

The old prosecutor's eyes scanned the stranger standing next to him and in the dim light of the balcony; he quickly decided that this man was not a politician. In fact, he was not too sure who, or what, he was. It seemed as if he had been, until now, lost in time and magically appeared on the balcony.

The man standing next to Charles "Chuck" McCracken was dressed all in black. His black vest covered a perfectly pressed black buttoned-up shirt, and his sharply creased black trousers had no ripples or wrinkles. There was nothing out of place on this man. Not a wrinkle, not a hair on his head, nothing. He was impeccable, immaculate.

His features were dark, he wore on his face, a finely trimmed beard, closely framing a perfectly chiseled face, dark, piercing black eyes staring straight ahead, emotionless, expressionless. On his head, he wore a wide-brimmed black hat, pulled down to where his facial features were not easily seen, but still visible even in the dim evening light of the balcony. On his feet were highly polished black boots, buffed to a mirror shine. If you bent down and looked at them, you could see your reflection in them. He did not speak, answer Chuck, or even appear to hear his remarks.

Standing next to Charles "Chuck" McCracken was the quiet stranger in the black hat.

"I have a strange feeling that you ain't no horn blowing, ass–sucking politician or some jackleg who is peddling some dumb-ass charity cause," the tough and cagey old attorney told the quiet stranger.

"However, you are the biggest damn guy that I've seen in a long time, pal. Have me a feeling that we have met before, somewhere. Maybe, I am wrong. Even if I was stumble-ass drunk, be kinda hard to forget, a guy like you."

Chuck now positively recalled the other meeting in another time and place and decided to keep his memories under wraps to see if the stranger commented on the past.

The quiet stranger in the black hat still did not answer. Instead, the stranger stared at Chuck out of the corner of his eyes. Chuck McCracken during his long career had been in the presence of a few ruthless criminals, murderers, thieves, and general scoundrels, many of them, who wished Chuck dead, chopped into little pieces and scattered to the wind, so he knew the definition of the word, "ominous."

At first, the lack of reaction from this dark stranger caused Chuck to stir a little uneasily. An ominous presence filled the air, as well as Chuck's soul when he first glanced at the immense man next to him. However, after a few brief moments of concern, Chuck relaxed. Something inside of him told him that this stranger and their encounter with each other this evening had a greater purpose and a good cause. Chuck might be gruff, cold, and at times crude, but above all, he was a very good and honest man. Gordon Tolland would not call him a friend or partner if he were anything but an honest man.

Chuck took a long sip from his drink. He sucked deeply on the cigarette and commented, "You only light 'em, but don't smoke 'em. You are smart."

The comment finally brought a reaction from the quiet stranger in the black hat. He nodded and then reached into his vest pocket and handed Chuck a small slip of paper. A slip, which proved to be a sales receipt.

Chuck placed his drink down on the ledge of the balcony wall and took the receipt from the quiet stranger. The cigarette dangled precariously from his lips until Chuck, sensing the importance of the paper that he now held, took one last drag, blew the smoke in the air and tossed the cigarette on the floor of the balcony. He ground it out with his shoe while carefully studying the receipt.

Chuck studied the paper and then produced a low whistle between his words, "Impressive. That is a big chunk of dough for a piece of jewelry. I think that I can connect some dots here. I am not sure who the hell you are, and for now, I might be better off not knowing that piece of information. Yet, I can tell you are a friend. If you are not a friend, then I had better have my track shoes on, cuz, you will squish me like a bug."

The dark stranger did not comment and when he remained silent, Chuck decided to confirm his memory, "I know that we have met before this. Am I correct? Have we met? I think we have done this before a long time ago. You would think that I would remember someone like you!"

Chuck looked at the quiet stranger in the black hat, the stranger tilted his hat back on his head just a bit more, smiled at the comments, and he finally spoke in a low, melodious voice, "Perhaps, we have met in the past. Time marches on and plays tricks with our minds. Yes, I think that a friend is as good a description of me, as any might be. Use the inscription that you read on the back of the bracelet to match up with the receipt and it will become clearer. I can tell you that the inscription is actually a lover's secret code for an address to a condominium unit. I will be here to help as much as I am able to, but my allowance for intervention is limited. The rest is up to you. Please do not give up, Chuck. Dig around, call in a few old favors with some old contacts, and please, you must do it very soon. Time will not wait."

The quiet stranger in the black hat looked up at the night sky. His eyes scanned the clear darkness and he smiled, and then spoke, "There is much to do and the night closes in."

Chuck nodded and mumbled, "Thanks a lot, big guy. Gotcha. If ya know me, then ya know that I don't give up too easily. I can't stand crooks, connivers, chiselers, and thieves."

"We share many common thoughts and opinions, Chuck. That is what I am counting upon," the quiet stranger in the black hat said as he smiled. He then tipped his hat, turned, and walked briskly away. Charles McCracken stood and watched as the quiet stranger in the black hat moved quickly along the stone floor of the balcony. The stranger walked down the steps of a long staircase and disappeared from his view. Chuck did not move, and he carefully listened until he could no longer hear the click of the metal tips of his boots upon the stairs.

Chuck reached for another cigarette, picked up his drink and mumbled, "Well now, shit, that was super damn, friggin' weird, but once more, damn glad he is a good guy. Knew he was. An allowance for intervention, huh? What in the hell does that mean? Who the hell is that guy?"

While pondering the quiet stranger's instructions and

words, as well as all that was happening, Chuck sipped the remainder of his drink. He then returned inside to the mass of people, wandered around until he found Gordon, politely excused them from a conversation and pulled Gordon aside.

The old attorney corralled his friend and leaned in to tell him, "Say, Gordy, I am going to call it an early night. I have had a bit too much Scotch to drive. One of them nights for me. Sucked down too much liquid courage. Can I borrow your limo and Jimmy to drive me home? I will send Jimmy back here, and maybe we can pick my car up tomorrow."

"No sweat, Chuck. Sure, please be safe. Jimmy will work it out to return here in the morning to pick up your car."

Gordon did not question his old friend, and the truth was that Chuck was not even close to being too tipsy to drive. The old attorney could hold his liquor, but Chuck whipped up a quick excuse in order to borrow the knowledge and services of Mr. James "Jimmy" Reeves. Jimmy served as a driver and bodyguard to Gordon Tolland and he had been an employee for both of them for many years. He was older now, but Jimmy was still tough as nails, big and strong. Jimmy served in the military, a marksman and legendary crack shot in the United States Marine Corps, a combat veteran from multiple overseas conflicts, a man who had dealt with his share of bullet dodging, and above all, he was brave, faithful, honest, and trustworthy. Jimmy Reeves was part of the team, and Gordon and Chuck trusted him with their lives.

Literally.

When the Night Closes In

Part 4

Back on the Trail

As Chuck sat next to their old friend, bodyguard and limo driver, Jimmy Reeves, and they made their way through the dark city streets, Chuck still pondered the strange events of the evening, the words of the quiet stranger in the black hat, and he tried very hard to put it together. He did have a thought, and Jimmy might be just the person he needed to help him.

"Say, Jimmy . . . I think that you know this old city as well as anyone does. Remind me, buddy, how long have you been driving around here?"

"Over fifteen years, Mr. McCracken. In fact, since I returned to this world from the Marine Corps. Been drivin' and protectin' you, Mr. Tolland, and your wives for a long time, since youse guys were practicin' attorneys and prosecutors. Protected Mr. Tolland Senior too. Yup, know every road, alleyway, street and corner, here and over there too."

"I bet. If I asked you to tell me, where there might be a condominium complex that has streets, which have the names of all different types of trees . . . well, off the top of your head, could you tell me if it exists around here? Chances are that it is a fancy joint, and it is not some slum dump."

Without hesitation, Jimmy answered quickly, "That's a slam dunk, Mr. McCracken. The Arboretum. All the streets in the Arboretum have street names like trees. You know . . . Oak Way, Maple Drive, and Ash Court and so on and so forth. Get it? The Arboretum and trees. It is kinda stupid soundin' but it is fancy. Super, high-end condominium units, so I guess the name is weird and eccentric. Word is that the mob built it and all the high rollers from the families own the joints. I pick up a few fares there when I am hackin' in a cab for a bud of mine and usually on those rides—I don't ask no questions."

Chuck smiled,, and he leaned back in the seat.

"Nice, Jimmy. Say, if you ever need extra dough, please, then just ask me for it. I might need you to give up any part-time gigs for a little while. Am thinkin' that we are back on the trail, my old friend. I am gonna need ya to re-up for another tour or two."

''Gotcha. I am a Marine. The only one way the tour ever ends, and that is when they plant me. You know that I am in."

"Good. Perfect. Say, can we go there? I need to go to a unit with the number one-sixty-eight, but I do not know the street name."

"Now?"

"Yes, now, and keep this one between you and me for now. I will tell Gordy when I can. This complex is a fancy mob joint, huh? So, does it have high security and gates? Can we get in?"

Jimmy took his eyes off the road for just a second so that Chuck could catch the wry smile on his face.

"Already told ya that I am in, but sumthin' tells me that we are already on a case, Mr. McCracken. Like the old days. I don't ask no questions, but I will tell ya that this fancy complex, it has a gate and a security guard. It might cost us a few bucks, but we can git in."

Chuck smiled as he playfully punched Jimmy on the

shoulder.

"Yup, just like the old times, Jimmy."

Jimmy pulled the limo up to a security gate in front of the condominium complex. A security guard swung the window of the guard shack open and stared into the driver's door of the limo, as Jimmy pushed the button for the window to roll down.

"Hey, Mike! Long time, no see!"

"Hey, Jimmy! Thought you gave up, retired and went to Florida."

"No, still drivin'. Ya know that I can't quit yet. Say, I got me a nice fare, but I was a dumb ass and wrote the number down but not the street name. I do not want to call them and let them know that I am a dumb ass. Hopin' there is only one unit with the number one-sixty-eight."

Mike laughed and smiled as he playfully leaned back and rubbed his chin, while saying, "Well, there is, but you know my memory is failing, Jimmy and my. . .."

Jimmy handed Mike twenty dollars and said, while peeling off an additional twenty dollars and handing it to Mike, "Here ya go. A memory booster. Appreciate if ya take your eye off the security cameras for a bit of time too and don't pay much attention to us poking around for our fare."

Mike smiled, reached over and pushed the button to lift up the gate, while he said, "Oh, I see. That type of fare, huh? Be careful, lots of uptight guys around here. I don't need no gunshots tonight and you kickin' thug's asses. One-sixty-eight-Birch Road. Two lefts and one right."

Jimmy pulled the limo slowly along, and when they circled the condominium's units; they spotted the unit number of one-sixty-eight, brightly shining under a porch light.

Chuck leaned over and told Jimmy, "Stop here, Jimmy. Move on down the road with the limo. I do not want to get too close. Keep your head on a swivel, Jimmy. Ya packin'?"

Jimmy did not answer Chuck's question. Instead, he smiled, and tapped his shoulder to indicate the location of his weapon.

"Good. I will go around back, where the parking is, and catch up to you down the road a little. If ya hear shit blowin' up, then come save my old ass."

Jimmy nodded, stopped the car, shut off the headlights and let Chuck out. Chuck silently and carefully made his way around the rows of units and, just as he suspected, he found dedicated parking spaces for each of the condominium units, all neatly tucked under an open carport for protection. The security cameras were monitoring the area, but Chuck knew that Mike, the security officer, was happily looking the other way. After all, Mike just made an easy forty bucks.

Chuck scanned the parking slot numbers assigned to the units and when he found number one-sixty-eight, he carefully noted the make and model of the expensive sports car that occupied the slot. Taking a notepad and pen from his suit jacket, he wrote down the license plate information for the car, glanced inside, and made mental notes of what he saw and observed.

A quick glance in the back seat and Chuck exclaimed, "Hello! What is this on the back seat?"

Chuck pressed his eyes up close to the glass in an effort to peer into the darkness. How he wished he had his pocket flashlight with him, but instead, he pulled his cellphone out of his pocket, pressed the dial buttons, and used the light from the device to cast a meager shadow upon the back seat. There, sitting happily upon the back seat, was a jewelry case, the type of expensive, high-end case, which a diamond bracelet would fit very neatly inside and provide for a stunning presentation. In addition to the spent jewelry box sitting on the seat were packs of bank deposit slips. Chuck did not need to have more light or zoom in any closer, in order to know that those deposit slips were for an account in the name of Senator Gordon Tolland. Even in the dim light, he could see the last name printed in block letters. He was now rather easily able to connect the dots in this horrible mess.

Chuck sighed and shook his head.

To strangers and those who had something to hide, Chuck McCracken gave a perception of being cold and often gruff, but to his close friends and those people who he loved, it was a different story.

Chuck cared deeply for his friend, and he shut his cellphone screen off, looked around to make sure he was still under cover, and mumbled to only the darkness, "I have seen it too many times. I swear. These bad guys all get cocky, they get sloppy and leave a trail a mile long. Shit. This really sucks. San Francisco, my ass. I knew it. Gordon is like a damn elephant. Guy never forgets shit. He is sharper than my gorgeous wife's nipples are. Damn, how the wrong woman in your life can drag ya down. This is gonna crush, Gordy."

The next day, in his home office, Chuck McCracken had made a number of telephone calls. Just as he did the previous evening, when he and Jimmy relived old times, he did exactly what the quiet stranger in the black hat had advised him to do.

He called in a number of favors.

First, he had a police contact run the license plate on the expensive sports car, and then, he called a contact to check into the actual deed holder or lease signer on a certain condominium unit located at one-sixty-eight, Birch Road in the Arboretum. Now, he just needed them to call him back, and Chuck felt that he had all that he required to put this messy puzzle together. Time was ticking hard now; he knew the state senate was convening shortly and the vote for Land-Gate was on the day's agenda. He did not want to make a hair trigger mistake, without all the facts and incorrectly influence Gordon. Not when the stakes were this high. Some of the details he will have to guess at and gather later, such as that smug-faced Senator Buckwald's finances. He would need to be in a high place to poke around those accounts. He could just feel that the senator was crooked and on the take.

Chuck looked up from his desk and paperwork, and he had a fleeting thought . . . maybe, he would give that state attorney general position a good, hard, look. Chuck mumbled aloud, "Damn, retirement is just another word for boredom. Plus, I can't stand crooks, connivers, chiselers, and thieves."

He smiled and then called out to his wife in the next room, "Hey, Michelle darlin'! Can you mix me a double Scotch, baby doll? Please. Make it neat."

"Too early! It is only eleven in the morning, Chuck. What are you working on that has you on edge?"

"Ah, please, bring it on in here, along with your gorgeous ass. C'mon in and hand it to me, would ya? As a preemptive measure, I already put my name on the donor list for a new liver. I gotta think, what is it going to matter?"

A few minutes later, Michelle McCracken walked through the doorway of Chuck's office, carrying the drink. She sighed as she set a double Scotch poured neat in front of her husband. He smiled as he picked it up and sipped it. Michelle leaned over and gently kissed her husband as he warmly embraced her.

He whispered to her as he gently rubbed his hand over the curves of, and then patted her backside, "Thanks, baby doll and you do have a great ass."

She pushed her husband away playfully and her tone then grew serious as she stood over Chuck and scanned the maze of papers on his desk.

"I know you too well, Charles McCracken. The humor is to offset some pain. The drink is to numb it. This is as if we have gone back in time. Is this really retirement for us? Here, I thought I would be floating on some sailboat in an ocean bay somewhere, topless and sunbathing, while you enjoyed a double Scotch neat." Michelle sighed and then, after catching her breath, she asked, "What is happening, Chuck? Seriously. Please, Chuck, tell me."

Chuck waved in the air, while still sipping the drink and he said, "All in due time on the sailboat and check on the topless part. Most likely bottomless at some point too. Seriously. We have some grave trouble to work through here. Trouble that will hurt someone very near and dear to both of us. Hurt him quite bad. And, if that phone does not ring soon, it is going to become a lot more serious and I will be sucking down a few more Scotches. It has been so strange the last few days, these feelings, it is as if someone or something has been guiding me along the way."

The concern enveloped Michelle McCracken's face, because she knew that her husband voided his brief retirement for a serious reason, and not for some trivial matter just to pass the time with.

"You were always intuitive, my love."

"No, I mean, yes, but this is very different. I am not this intuitive. Sometimes, you cannot explain things, but how this has all fallen into place is quite remarkable. As if an unseen, hand has guided me. Then last night, I met this stranger. A big guy, no, wrong . . . that is a poor description. He was friggin' immense. The biggest damn man, I think that I ever met. A stranger, large and dark, but a good guy. The stranger, he told me things. His quiet power still goes through me. It was controlling, omnipresent. Very strange."

"A stranger, dear Chuck? You never met him before, last night?"

"That is the funny thing. I know that somewhere, we

have met before. I have a memory of this guy. In fact, it was almost the same scene. I think that this time it replayed a bit differently. Who knows? The mind plays crazy tricks on you sometimes."

Michelle now knew that Chuck was deeply involved in investigating something of a criminal nature, and when Michelle put the playful joking aside, she had an idea of whom it might involve.

"You were out with Jimmy last night after the event. He dropped you off so late. My guess is that this has something to do with, Gordy."

"Yes, it does."

"Oh, Chuck. I am so sorry."

"Don't be sorry, baby doll. Evil people and assholes chart their own courses in their lives. Guys like, Gordy. and Jimmy, and me, we hunt them down and make 'em pay. All I need right now, is your love and support."

"Well, you always have that." Michelle walked behind Chuck's chair. She leaned over and wrapped her arms around her husband's shoulders and held him for a long time. Chuck reached up, held his wife's hands, and embraced them tightly. Even after over thirty years of marriage, the two of them remained deeply in love. They were a team and they always would be a team.

Ten minutes later, as the tension grew thicker, and the Scotch flowed harder, the telephone on Chuck's desk finally rang. It was his police contact, confirming what Chuck already felt he knew. The sports car license plate came back to Mr. Richard Stafford. The same Richard Stafford that supposedly wrote the "independent" report that Gordon studied so deeply for weeks upon weeks, but Gordon was too smart, not to know that it somehow was not very independent at all. The same Richard Stafford, who Jennifer Tolland might know from some meetings here and there, but the not-for-profit organization that Mrs. Tolland served on the board of directors for, was all too happy to recommend for writing the suspicious report for the project. The same, Richard Stafford, whose car's rear seat coincidentally, had an empty jewelry case and a pack of Gordon Tolland's deposit slips sitting upon the seat.

One more piece was all that Chuck needed, and then he would be confident enough to call Gordon, and tell him to vote no, and have a very painful discussion with his beloved friend. Shortly after the first call came the final piece of the puzzle. The telephone rang as his real estate contact carefully spelled out the name of the person who owned condo-unit number one-sixty-eight Birch Road. Chuck wrote the name of the famous mobster that seemed to be untouchable on the pad. The actual name of the owner was a well-known front company for the mobster's organization. When Chuck heard the registered name, he could easily do the translation. It was a bogus name that he had heard many times before in his career, and he now knew who the actual owner was. He carefully scrawled the name of Tony Michanetti upon the pad, thanked his contact, and hung up the telephone.

Chuck nervously stirred the remaining Scotch in his glass with his pointer finger and mumbled, "Someday, Tony . . . I told you we would meet again, and someday, I am gonna get ya ass. I swear. I can't stand crooks, connivers, chiselers, and thieves, and we protect our own. Gordy is our own."

Downing the last of the whiskey, Chuck dialed Gordon's cellphone number.

Gordon answered on the first ring, whispering into the phone, "Hello, Chuck. Look, going to vote on the bill now. I really cannot talk."

"Gordy, listen to me. Carefully! Vote no. I repeat, vote no. Please, buddy. Please, listen carefully to me. Ya gotta vote no! Go with your original gut feelings."

"What? Why? I need to tell you that after we returned home from the event, I had a lovely evening with Jennifer last night. We talked about it for a long time. I think that I have put aside my reservations. She made some very good points. . .."

"PLEASE, PLEASE, PLEASE, DO NOT VOTE YES!" Chuck screamed and cut his friend off. "Listen to me carefully, my friend. Vote no. This is a set-up, and it is going to hurt you a great deal, but I can tell you all the disgusting details after the vote. Please, trust me, Gordy. Of all the people in the world, you do trust me, don't you?"

"Yes, of course, I do, Chuck. Without any questions or doubts."

"Then, please vote no, get the hell outta there and come over to our house. It will be better to tell you the details here. Michelle, Jimmy, and I will take good care of you. I will explain. . .."

When the Night Closes In

Conclusion

Justice

Two years later, Attorney General Charles "Chuck" McCracken stood at a podium in the old city's main courtroom. He was just finishing commenting during a press conference about the final convictions and sentencing of the participants in the Land-Gate scandal.

"Former New Jersey State Senator Buckwald, Richard Stafford, and the former Mrs. Gordon Tolland, all received what I felt were fair sentences. They will be in jail for a long time, but eligible for parole in a few years. Considering all that happened after the senate voted no on the sale, it is remarkable what came to light. You know . . . what the impact could have been. The fact that when the news came down from the feds that the interstate would roll right along the front of the parcels, the state eventually sold some of the land for three times the estimated price. All of that, besides, the parklands that we established, in order to protect the natural areas. Then, of course, the money made when the sale finally went through to legitimate and established developers. What a damn mess this could have been! Yet, Senator Gordon Tolland held the line, and the senator voted with his heart to stop the crooked deal. His no vote swayed others to vote no, and the rest is now history. In the end, it all turned out quite well. It was complex, deeply rooted and amazing. I would say, in light of all of this that all of these bums got off pretty easy. I am okay with the plea bargain and hand slap for the young woman, Ms. Lisa Mackworth. I hope that she gets her life in order. The bogus corporation and supposed investors, well, not too much, we could do there. Now, they know that we are watching. As far as, Tony Michanetti goes. . .."

Chuck turned and faced the camera, and his demeanor grew intense.

With a scowl on his face and a purposeful and intense finger pointed at the camera, Chuck proclaimed, "Sooner or later, smart ass, we will nail ya. I have friends too. One special one comes to mind. You have no idea who he is, and together, what we can do! Justice, in the end, will always prevail. That is my mission and I have a feeling it is my friend's mission too! We both can't stand crooks, connivers, chiselers, and thieves!"

After fielding a few questions, Chuck McCracken, in keeping with his usual impatient behavior, waved his hands in the air and called an abrupt end to the press conference.

All the time to the chuckles of the crowd and the press reporters, who were now familiar with his famous grouchy demeanor, Chuck spouted off, "I need a double Scotch neat. In fact, it is five minutes past eleven in the morning, so I am overdue now! How do you people manage to ask me the same stupid, dumb ass questions, over and over and waste my time, while I need to be hitting the streets to find the crooks, connivers, chiselers, and thieves?"

Chuck descended the podium and shook hands with a few supporters offering congratulations on the news, and then he met his wife and his faithful driver, sidekick and bodyguard, Mr. Jimmy Reeves.

A uniformed police officer walked up to Attorney General McCracken and asked Chuck, "Sir, do you need a police escort for you and Mrs. McCracken? My commander instructed me to check with you. He said that things might be a little stirred up right now."

Chuck patted the officer gently on the back and with a smile, Chuck told the officer, "Yeah, I guess they are. I tend to do that. Thanks, but nah, got me a Jimmy Reeves. No offense, but one Jimmy is all we need, and it is worth a battalion of youse guys. Thanks."

The officer looked over at Jimmy Reeves and he smiled, nodded, and walked away.

Jimmy's reputation was quite well known.

"Well, Chuck, I guess I am still a few years away from that sailboat ride," Michelle said as she leaned in for a kiss from her husband.

"Afraid so, baby doll, but ya still got a dynamite ass and our nights are still explosive."

"Too much info, boss," Jimmy covered his ears playfully as he listened to the banter.

"Jimmy, please pull the limo around back, would you, buddy? You will join us tonight, at our table at Nous Somme Du Soleil. Lots of booze, food, and celebratin'. Might need a damn driver for our driver."

"Honey, Gordy called to congratulate you. He said he had an appointment on Capitol Hill, but that he will catch up to you later."

"Thanks, Michelle. I will call him. Now that he is the big shot, United States Senator Tolland, I will have to make an appointment to catch up to him. Bet ya, gorgeous ass though, that, when I visit, I will still put my feet on his desk. . .."

Chuck's words and thoughts drifted off as his eyes caught a man standing in a far corner of the room. Quietly, the man was watching from afar, and Chuck could not help but smile at the sight of him. His wife and Jimmy caught his eyes and they too turned and looked in the direction of the man who had captured Chuck's eyes.

"Say, Jimmy, take my baby doll, and bring her to the car. I will catch up to you." He gently tugged at his friend and bodyguard and whispered to Jimmy, "You are packin,' right?"

"Sure boss, all is well."

"From here on in, keep your head on a swivel, Jimmy. We did not make any friends today."

"Understood, boss. We never did, and I guess we never will. I did not expect that to change. I did not sign back up to make friends, I signed back up to make a difference. I know, this here guy, who always tells me that he can't stand crooks, connivers, chiselers, and thieves! Besides, if ya never stood for anything in your life, then you are everyone's best friend," Jimmy said as he smiled, and Chuck patted him on the back. Jimmy took Mrs. McCracken by the hand and started to lead her out the door.

"C'mon, Mrs. McCracken. Stay right next to me until we get to the limo."

"I will, Jimmy. Is that someone that you know, dear Chuck?" Michelle asked her husband as Jimmy took her by the arm. "He is a very big man, good-looking too." She smiled at her observation.

"Yeah, he is a friend, baby doll. A very good friend."

Chuck nodded, made sure that his wife was safe with Jimmy, and then he walked over in the direction of the quiet stranger in the black hat. He extended his hand and the quiet stranger took it and they shook hands. Immediately, Chuck felt an incredible warmth and comfort come over his body.

"I knew that you would show up today. You had better have shown up, especially after I spouted off like some kind of a drunken fool about my special friend! The worst part is that I ain't even bombed yet. Soon, but not yet. I wish we could've nailed Tony Michanetti. Got him in my sights, but he is a slick one. Slipped by me on this one. Oh well, I won't quit on him. I would ask ya for a match, but we have been down those roads a few times before, and even the big blowhard chief of all of state law enforcement cannot smoke in here."

Chuck looked around and pointed at a "No Smoking" sign mounted on the wall, as if to confirm the fact that he could not smoke.

"I do need to thank you. Thank you, for being a friend. Gordon means the world to us. That young man is going to be a positive influence in a negative world. Hell, Michelle and I never had our own children, so we love him like a son, and Jimmy loves him like a brother."

The quiet stranger in the black hat only smiled and nodded his head, but as expected, he did not say a word.

"There was so much more to this than it appears. Now to me, your involvement makes such sense. A corrupt senator taking mob dough, affairs, payoffs, mobsters, a drug addict who is rehabbing her life, all the way to the preservation of natural lands. Well, it is kinda amazing. Funny, how Jennifer musta really loved that punk, Stafford. They got married before they all headed off to prison. True love is friggin' weird. However, most of all, I see now that above all that wild nonsense, it was to protect Gordon. He is destined for great things and you already know that. Don't ask me how you already know that, however, I can safely say that you ain't from around here. I know a Jersey guy and sorry, buddy, but you do not make the cut. I am right, ain't I? Plus, ya knew that I was bullshitting when I faked that I did not recall meeting you the first time . . . ya know, when we first met. How do you forget a guy like you are? Ya was planting the seeds. Don't you already know all of this shit that I am rambling on 'bout here?"

The quiet stranger in the black hat nodded again, and this time, he gently placed his hand upon Chuck's shoulder.

"Here, I am ramblin' on endlessly and you just stand there and remain silent. You sure don't say much, do ya?"

The quiet stranger still did not answer the excited and

intense Charles "Chuck" McCracken. Instead, he stared a little more intently at the attorney general. Despite the intenseness of the stare, the quiet stranger's eyes were dark, but softer in their glow. Chuck found it hard not to focus on the quiet stranger's eyes.

Chuck looked away for a brief moment and continued to explain, "I also see that in this grand plan of yours . . . part of it was to wrap my old ass up within this attorney general bullshit."

The quiet stranger, once again, nodded gently. He still did not speak, but his nod confirmed Chuck's supposition that his new position was indeed, part of the plan.

Chuck mumbled, "I knew it. So, this ain't the end. We are gonna work together on some other adventures. Well, I am gonna need you . . . Jimmy, Gordy, and I . . . we can't do all this stuff by ourselves. Too much, damn evil out there. Plus, I can't stand crooks, connivers, chiselers, and thieves, but I guess ya know that too. Somehow, I know that you will always be there, if and when, I need ya to be. Is that your mission, to ensure justice, my dark, quiet friend? To make sure that good, always prevails?"

The quiet stranger in the black hat leaned back. He adjusted his hat, and he fully exposed his face to Charles, who marveled at how his dark eyes sparkled and reflected such profound hope and joy.

The stranger finally spoke, "Amongst many missions, I do have the task to make sure that justice prevails. With the assistance of outstanding men such as Gordon, Jimmy Reeves, and you are, it always will be that way. Now, until the end of all time. Always remember, that there are more of us, who seek justice and protect good will, than there are of them, who seek to destroy it. Charles, I know that out of all good people on this planet, I do not have to tell you this. However, as a reminder, do not fear, never be afraid and above all, do not back down. Tony Michanetti is able to bypass your laws and utilize loopholes within them to avoid justice. Occasionally, my allowance for intervention expands and when it does, I only answer to one law and it has no loopholes. I am always watching from the shadows, turning the light on brightly, whenever the night closes in."

"Intervene away, dark friend. It sounds as if we are now a team. Honestly, I am damn sure that there ain't anyone else that I would want on my team other than Gordy, Jimmy, and you. Do ya have a name?"

The quiet stranger in the black hat did not answer the question; instead, he smiled, tipped his hat, and then turned and walked briskly away.

Chuck mumbled his thoughts aloud, in his typical gruff fashion, "I guess not. What a dumb ass question for me to ask. This guy don't need no name. He sure does not say too much, but when he speaks, he really means it."

Chuck scratched the top of his flattop haircut and continued to watch the stranger's exit, while Chuck continued to mumble thoughts aloud, "Sure, knows how to make a quick exit too. That is the second time that he mentioned this allowance for intervention, so he answers to something or . . . someone. Weird. Still not too sure, who the hell he is, or where he comes from. I think that I am better off not knowing, but I am damn sure glad that he is on our side."

Attorney General Charles "Chuck" McCracken could not help but smile, while he stood and watched as the quiet stranger in the black hat moved quickly along the floor of the room. While the stranger briskly walked away, his boots made a loud and distinctive clicking noise as he moved along the wooden floor. Chuck continued to watch and smile, until the quiet stranger went out the front door. He disappeared from his view, and the click of the metal tips of his boots upon the floor, became a distant echo.

THE END

The Circle of Life

For thirty-two years, Mr. Eddie Bagley worked the second shift. He closed the machine shop down, and Eddie carefully watched until the chip sweepers cleaned all the metal dust and chips out from under the lathes. Eddie always made sure they picked up all the chips.

He encouraged the young apprentices that worked as chip sweepers by telling them, "Sweeping chips up is how I started in this business." After that prelude, Eddie had a long speech that he gave to all the chip sweepers. "If you work hard as a chip sweeper, then you can work your way up. Maybe, someday, when I am gone, you can even run the shop. You have to remember that those chips are lost profit sitting there on the floor. Gather them all and put them in the chip box. When it is full, we will have a fork truck come and take it away to the loading dock. We recycle it all and get some of our money back. Every penny saved might mean a raise for you someday."

He never worked the graveyard shift. There was no need to, because that was when the shop maintenance crew performed all the maintenance, inspection, and repairs on the machines. Six hundred and seventy-three machines, and Eddie managed them all.

Besides, the graveyard shift was not a production shift, and Eddie was a production guy. Junking parts, creating scrap out of good metal, and looking around for something to work on, was not in his vocabulary.

After working on the second shift for all of those years, his boss promoted him to a floor general foreman, and he moved to the first shift. He did not know what to do with himself! It took his body a solid year to adjust to actually being awake during these new hours. It had been difficult on his family, Eddie working the second shifts all of those years, but they worked around it. Eddie made it up to his family on the weekends; he spent as much time as he could with his wife and two children. A boy and a girl and a good wife and despite his dedication to his job, his family came first. Eddie worked it all out.

He had no complaints.

No complaints until the company told him that it was time for Eddie to retire. Eddie Bagley had worked the first shift for another fifteen years. Forty-seven years of working, and now Eddie was done. At first, he was upset, his health was still good, and he felt as if he was still a valuable and contributing worker and an important person for the company to have. Eddie was still young; he began his career in the machine shop while he was a teenager, right out of trade school as one of those valued chip sweepers. Eddie was still only sixty-three years old and a few ticks more or thereabouts.

He felt he could still go a few more years. Besides, what would he do now? Eddie Bagley was the longest serving employee in the history of the entire company. Even the original owners had retired and moved on, but Eddie remained. His employee badge was number fifty-five. No one in the entire company had a lower number.

In this modern world, the attitudes in business operations and the manner of how they treat and respect employees had changed drastically from when Eddie first started sweeping chips.

After some tears, a big retirement party, a wristwatch with a happy inscription, a plaque for his wall, and too many boring speeches and not enough beer, the cheers from the attendees rose to coax Eddie into saying a few words. The crowd, his family, and management, pressed Eddie to say a few words and despite the fact that he did not want to speak, after some prodding, he slowly walked up to the podium in front of the room and spoke.

"Thank you for everything and most of all, thank you for keeping me around here for forty-seven damn years. I am sure gonna miss it and all of you, too. Love the roar of the machines in the morning . . . when they first start up. I really do not want to go, but everyone tells me that it is some line of bullshit about the circle of life. All I can say is that, I gave it my best every day, and I worked as hard as I could to earn the money that ya paid me. As far as working on the machine shop floor, I will leave you with what I told my first boss here all those years ago, when he finally moved me from chip sweepin' to runnin' a twelve-inch swing turret lathe. I told him that I would give you my best swings at all the pitches, every, single day. I won't let ya down. I hope that I kept my promise. Think I did. I also told him to tell them all around here that Bagley is the name. Tell them all that, I don't jam 'em, break 'em or scrap 'em."

With that humble speech from a master tradesman, the party was over and so was Eddie Bagley's career in the machine shop.

He was teary eyed the next day when he did not have to rise early in the morning and drive into work. He felt a bit empty inside and hollow. Something significant seemed to be missing, a great deal out of place in his life.

After all—that is a very long time to work.

His wife was quiet, calm and wise, and when she noticed her husband struggling, she calmly told him, "Eddie dear, it will be fine. It is just the circle of life, my darling. You have worked so hard for so long, now it is time for you to relax and enjoy life. We have been married now for fifty-five years. Our children are all grown and married now and with families of their own. The grandchildren will visit all the time. It should be a time of great joy in our lives. It is more than time for you to relax. Maybe, we can sit together and watch the sunsets on the porch, while we sip some red wine. Wouldn't that be so nice?"

Eddie thought how red wine gave him a damn headache and made him have to pee all night long, yet he reluctantly agreed. Deep in the back of his mind, he knew that the machine shop would never leave him. His work was too deeply rooted inside of his mind and inside of his soul.

It was a part of him forever.

Besides, who was watching the chip sweepers now? You have to make sure they recover all the precious metal dust and chips and recycle them. Those pieces represent lost profit. A profit that would be a shame to lose when it is so easy to recover.

Mr. Eddie Bagley needed to let go, but that is no easy task and it would take some time. . ..

Time went on and Mr. Eddie Bagley went about his retired life. However, he never was quite the same. Whenever there were family get-togethers at Christmas or Thanksgiving or any event in between, Eddie would tell, as his family would rather teasingly say, "Machine shop stories." Eddie would get a lick in his eye, or sit on the edge of his seat, when his son or his son-in-law, or for that matter, anyone, would tell stories of their particular work or career. It inspired such memories for him and returned his mind once again to those times he missed so much.

Eddie had very little in the way of hobbies, a little gardening here and there, and he would catch a football game or baseball game on the television, but he would grow bored rather quickly. He had a few old-time work friends that he occasionally would meet and visit with, tip a few beers or talk a little sports action with, but he was not, by any means, an overly social person. Cordial and polite, yes, social, not really. Eddie missed them more for work relationships than he missed them on friendly terms.

About five years after his retirement, the Bagleys moved out of the house that they had lived in, raised a family in, and spent most of their life living in together. Mrs. Bagley convinced Eddie that it was time to sell their big house.

"It is the circle of life, my darling. You do not need to mow all that grass or trim all those shrubs or tend to such a large garden. We need something smaller, with less maintenance, and a smaller porch to sit on and watch the sunsets, while we sip our red wine."

Eddie eventually agreed. It did make sense. They sold the old house and moved into a smaller house in a brand-new, senior–living subdivision, in some obscure town forty miles from where Eddie lived and worked for all of those years. Mr. Bagley thought how despite the change of porches from an old one to a new one that he still got a headache from red wine and it still made him get up all night and have to pee.

He read the newspaper here and there, and occasionally, he would notice in the obituaries, when some of his old friends had passed away. He did not attend the funerals, and it had been forever since they shared a beer. Eddie checked his old address book and work notebook for addresses, and he sent sympathy cards to the families. Eddie assumed that the letters arrived because they did not return to his mailbox.

There was not too much happening these days in the brand-new fresh home in the senior-living neighborhood. It was exactly as the salesperson who sold them the home had described to them with perfectly laid out streets, with cookie cutter homes stamped out of the same mold, lined up as far as the eye could see. All of these wonderful homes with the same look, the same lawns, even the damn mailboxes were identical. Yes, indeed, all of these homes, all carefree and maintenance-free too!

"Perfect," Eddie recalled the salesperson telling them as they signed on the dotted line.

Too perfect for guys like Eddie Bagley.

Guys like Eddie Bagley needed things to fix; they lived for breakdowns and for maintenance tasks. It kept them sharp and gave them a purpose.

Eddie puttered around in the new house, looking for things to try to keep him busy and his mind occupied. But honestly, there was not too much to do. The walls were all new and fresh, and a coat of paint was the last thing that they needed. Not even a faucet in the new house dripped, and the heat and air conditioning worked perfectly. Too perfect; so perfect that Eddie longed for them to malfunction, so it would give him an excuse to break out the tools and fix something. He did have a gutter and a downspout that clogged one afternoon in a thunderstorm. It was an emergency breakdown, and Eddie clamored into action for a whopping ten minutes or thereabouts.

His wife convinced him to sell his old pickup truck and buy a new one; something about the circle of life.

Now, he did not even have to change the oil anymore. Part of the sales deal was, as Eddie called them, "Some stupid-ass coupons" that gave Eddie free oil changes for the life of the vehicle. The best that Eddie could do was to vacuum the interior out, wash it every other day, and polish the hood.

At least, there were still trips to the supermarket, a trip or two to the local bank, some doctor visits, and the usual adventures at the dentist's office. He carried the trash out to the street once a week and the recycling container went out twice a month. Eddie wrote down the dates of the trash collections, on a calendar that he hung on the wall of his garage, right next to a shelf he put up to store the many cans of truck wax that he received for gifts on Christmas and on Father's Day. He also was in charge of making coffee in the morning and vacuuming the second-floor carpets. His wife vacuumed the first floor, but she could not carry the heavy vacuum cleaner up the stairs to do the second floor.

As he pushed the button to turn on the vacuum, Eddie said aloud, "Forty-seven damn years of running six hundred and seventy-three turret lathes, milling machines, grinders and parts scrubbers, and now, I get a shiver up my ass when I push buttons on coffee machines and vacuum carpets."

Oh well, it helped to pass the time. In addition to those exciting missions, there were weddings, birthdays, holidays, graduations, and with the happy times, came the unhappy times too. Along came the troubles, such as funerals, divorces, health scares and concerns, arguments between family members, children who moved across the country for employment, or for them to satisfy wanderlust, all the typical heartaches and family strife.

The circle of life. Then again, when you are a dreamer, it is actually quite easy.

"You should walk a bit more, Eddie. Maybe go around the subdivision. A little light exercise will do you a world of good. You are eighty-five years old now and the tests show a little heart leakage going on with a valve or two. It is not too serious, a little old age creeping in now, but you need some light exercise."

Eddie Bagley sat on an examination table and he listened to a doctor, who was half of Eddie's age, explain the results of his latest medical examination. Eddie could not help but notice the huge belly of the doctor overhanging his belt and as the doctor spoke, Eddie could pick up the distinctive odor of cigarettes on his body and breath.

"I guess I am nuthin' but a grand, old relic now, huh, Doc?"

"No, no, not really. It is all normal, Eddie, all part of the circle of life." Eddie shrugged his shoulders and thought about how there was not too much else to do these days.

Therefore, Eddie walked.

Around and around, he walked along the same streets; after all, it was a little interesting to see what was going on in the neighborhood. He walked in the cool weather, skipped the freezing days and the hot days, and he observed the same things over and over again. Same people to wave to, same dogs walking with the same people, same trees, same curbs and those same stupid identical mailboxes too. On occasion, his wife walked with him, but she was ten years younger than Eddie was, and she felt that she did not need to exercise as much. Eddie did not care one way or another. Sometimes, he enjoyed the quiet times better. He loved Mrs. Bagley with all of his heart, but sometimes, Eddie preferred the silence to any conversation. Eddie decided that he much preferred the loud whir of machines running in a machine shop.

Eddie always loved the roar of the machines in the morning when they first started up.

The first indication of something wrong with Mr. Eddie Bagley started innocently enough. Mrs. Bagley laughed at her husband when she discovered he was walking around with two left shoes and no right shoes on his feet. When Mrs. Bagley pointed it out to Eddie, she noticed that he at first did not even understand where he had gone wrong in his shoe selection, and then he too laughed. The two of them laughed it off because of a lack of sleep. As of late, Eddie was suffering from some insomnia. The occasional forgetfulness, his lack of focus and the insomnia, she chalked up to old age, and when she made sure that Eddie told his doctor about it, the doctor also told Eddie that he was not as young as he once was.

The incident that triggered a deeper investigation of what was occurring with the health of Mr. Eddie Bagley occurred when he went for one of his daily walks. Those same familiar streets, the same curbs, the same trees and yes, those identical mailboxes, suddenly became unfamiliar and Eddie found that he was lost. He wandered aimlessly, and nothing seemed to make any sense to him. When he did not return for hours upon hours, Mrs. Bagley grew frantic; she took Eddie's pickup truck and drove the streets of the subdivision all to no avail! She could not find Eddie anywhere!

Mrs. Bagley returned home to call the police and report the desperate situation, when the door opened and Eddie and a neighbor walked in the front hallway. The neighbor explained that he had spotted Eddie walking on the side of the road, miles away out on the main road that led into the subdivision and that poor Eddie seemed lost and extremely confused.

He kept telling the neighbor that he needed to go to the machine shop to work.

The sheer horror at the speed of which the disease progressed left doctors, loved ones, sons, daughters and Mrs. Bagley stunned and heartbroken. At first, the diagnosis of a mild case of Alzheimer's disease moved within a six-month period, to a moderate level, and within about one year and a half or just a little more, Mr. Eddie Bagley had reached a more progressive level of the wretched disease. Furthermore, there was that heart valve condition, and that was of some serious concern now too.

The doctors and nurses all told Mrs. Bagley, and their children and grandchildren, that Alzheimer's disease was a disease, which was worse in its effects on the loved ones and caregivers than it was on the victim of the disease. They all told Mrs. Bagley that Eddie did not have any pain, nor was he suffering at all.

Mrs. Bagley was not so sure.

To watch a man, who operated six hundred and seventy-three complex machines, and who led a team of expert machinists to produce intricate parts for jet aircraft for forty-seven years, now, unable to figure out a television remote control, or how to work a can opener, tore her very soul apart. Eddie Bagley was now a shell of a man, an emotionless human being, who often did not even know who his wife or children were. He knew or recalled very little, but one memory that remained remarkably intact was his career as a machinist.

Eddie could no longer drive; he was not even able to figure out how the door handles on his pickup truck operated, but Mrs. Bagley would pull the truck out of the garage on nice days and let Eddie try to wash it and wipe a rag along the hood. It kept him occupied, and almost every time he "washed" his truck, he mentioned how the trailer ball hitch on the rear lip of the bumper was rusty.

"I can make a new one on a lathe. I would load the stock and turn a new one in about an hour. Would make it out of a chunk of stainless, so it would never rust."

Mrs. Bagley would smile and admire how even in his terrible confusion and haze, the deeply embedded memories of a lifetime of craftsmanship remained and could surface. He often did not know her, but in his mind, he knew a lathe.

"We can buy a new hitch at the store for your truck, Eddie," Mrs. Bagley offered.

"Nope. Gonna make a good one on a lathe."

Eddie was a handful to take care of these days. Television was a temporary diversion. He could not operate the remote control, and his attention span was too short for him to concentrate on one show for very long. Mrs. Bagley had nursing care during the week to provide her with some respite. She loved her husband with all of her heart, but it was not only heart wrenching to observe his demise, but it exhausted her. To give her some peace of mind, as well as some much-needed rest, Mrs. Bagley had door alarms installed that would loudly sound and wake her, if Eddie decided to wander and escape. Despite pleas and desperate conversation from her children, friends and loved ones, she steadfastly refused to put him in a nursing home, until she just could no longer manage the situation.

She was close.

Yet, after these many years of marriage and love, she was going to hang on to her Eddie until the very end. Her children and loved ones admired her loyalty and her perseverance, but they worried at how long the situation could go on, until some kind of horrible incident occurred, or Mrs. Bagley's own health began to suffer.

Sometimes, the cruelness of this world is difficult to understand. How people such as Eddie Bagley could end up where they were at this moment in time is difficult to comprehend or to accept and understand. Eddie was now a mere shell of his former self, a man grasping to overcome the haze within his mind, lost in his own world and left to dwindle down and expire without joy or without dignity. On the other hand, does something, or someone, intervene on occasion, to bring things to light, to ease pain and shed light on the true meanings of why all of this suffering is allowed to exist in a world controlled by a loving God?

To restore the honor, to restore the pride, and to allow one last moment of joy and glory.

Door alarms are a grand idea, but only when you make sure that they are in the "on" position. Mrs. Bagley was sure that she switched the alarm on. The faithful wife always triple-checked it. Yet, during the night, the alarm, mysteriously and silently . . . moved to the "off" position.

It was as if an unseen hand guided the mechanism.

At two in the morning on a clear, late summer morning, Eddie Bagley walked out the front door to his home.

The door alarm did not sound.

He mumbled to himself, "It was time to go to work. Time to make that new hitch out of stainless steel for my truck."

He walked out the front door, while poor Mrs. Bagley soundly slept, exhausted from a particularly difficult day of taking care of her husband. Eddie walked and where he was walking to was of no concern to him. In his mind, he was going to work, and that is all that mattered. Out of the subdivision's winding roads, Eddie walked and out onto the main road he wandered. Once he was out on the main road, Eddie walked, he walked, and he walked.

In the cool morning air on the end of the main road, about one-half a mile away from where Eddie Bagley was walking, stood a very large man. He stood on a corner next to a bus stop at an intersection. The man looked up at the sky, and then he turned around and gazed at his surroundings. It was he, in some way, was confirming his whereabouts or his present location. The man's lean, tall, and muscular frame remained slightly concealed in the dark shadows of the early morning light. The streetlights glowed above him, and even if this was an intersection in the center of the town, there was very little traffic at this time of the morning. The county bus stopped here, and it did so on the hour. Right now, it was very close to the top of the hour.

The man standing on the corner was dressed all in black, he wore a black vest covering a perfectly pressed black buttoned-up shirt, and his sharply creased black trousers had not a single ripple or a wrinkle in them. There was nothing out of place on this man, not a wrinkle, not a hair on his head, nothing. He was impeccable, immaculate.

His features were dark, he wore on his face, a finely trimmed beard, closely framing a perfectly chiseled face, dark, piercing black eyes staring straight ahead, emotionless, expressionless. On his head, he wore a black hat, pulled down to where his facial features were not easily seen, but still visible. On his feet were highly polished black boots, buffed to a mirror shine. If you bent down and looked at them, you could see your reflection in them.

A man passed by, walking his dog in the early morning hours, and the dog-walker noticed the dark, tall man standing near the bus stop. He could not help but notice him; he was not the kind of man who blended in with his surroundings, even in the darkness. The dark stranger's handsome appearance and immense size proved to be a magnet; his features were striking and very captivating.

As the walker passed by with his dog, he mumbled, "Good morning" and smiled, while his dog tugged and tried hard to greet the man dressed all in black. His greeting seemed to fall upon deaf ears, as the dark stranger did not answer him or even acknowledge the greeting.

The man standing on the corner under the streetlight near the bus stop was the quiet stranger in the black hat. The quiet stranger looked up and down the street. It seemed as if he, was looking for someone; as if he knew that very shortly, someone would arrive, but he was not sure from which direction the person would be arriving.

Shortly after the dog-walker disappeared from the street corner, Eddie Bagley arrived at the same intersection where the quiet stranger waited. He arrived from the north side of the street and when he finally made it to the corner, Eddie stopped, wiped his brow, and he stood there for a few seconds while catching his breath.

It had been a long walk and his heart was not too good at pumping.

Eddie then looked deeply into the eyes of the quiet stranger in the black hat. The quiet stranger in the black hat smiled at Eddie, but he did not say a single word.

Eddie smiled back.

"That's a damn nice hat," Eddie said while pointing a finger at his hat and studying the stranger through the darkness and in his hazy mind. "I hope this is where the damn bus stops. I got to go to work. I was gonna take my truck, but I decided to walk. The doctor told me to walk a lot. You sure are a big man. I think you are the biggest guy that I have ever seen. Are you going to work too?"

The quiet stranger smiled and finally spoke, "Yes, Eddie. We are going to go to work today. Together."

"Well, now that is good. Say, do I know you? I am in charge of the shop. I thought I knew everyone who worked there. What do you do in the shop for me?"

"A long time ago you knew me, Eddie. We have been together many times, for many years. Right now, for you, today, I am a chip sweeper, Eddie."

Eddie smiled widely and patted the quiet stranger on the back, while he almost shouted, "Good, good, I am gonna need you, today! That is how I started out! Sure, are dressed fancy for a chip sweeper, but hell, times change and you gotta start somewhere. Let's go then, big man. Off to work! Got to make a new hitch for my truck. Gonna make it out of stainless, so it doesn't rust. Can't wait to hear the roar of the machines when they first start up. Love that sound."

The two men stood on the corner and waited for the bus to arrive. When it did arrive, they climbed the bus steps and the quiet stranger reached inside his vest, pulled out a few bus tokens and dropped them in the bus meter.

Other than the bus driver, there were no other riders on the bus, but Eddie proudly announced to the bus driver, "We are going to work. Got to make a part on the lathe for my truck! Damn hitch is all rusty. Gonna make it out of stainless."

The bus driver looked over at the quiet stranger in the black hat, who only gently tipped his hat and smiled, but he did not say a word. The driver followed his eyes and knew where the quiet stranger was leading him. He nodded and smiled as he pulled the lever to close the bus door.

"Is that so, old timer? Going to go to work, huh? Good for you. Sounds as if stainless is the way to go."

Eddie was satisfied with the driver's reply, he quietly sat next to the stranger, and the only time that he spoke during the bus ride, was to mention the fact that he forgot to pack his lunch pail, and he hoped that the cafeteria was open today, so they could eat lunch together.

The bus rolled along for a few miles and the quiet stranger in the black hat carefully watched the cityscape as it passed by the window. When he spotted a certain location, he reached up and pulled the alarm line to indicate to the driver to stop at the next corner. The bus gently pulled into the curb and the driver looked back at Eddie and the quiet stranger in the black hat.

The driver seemed puzzled at the location request as he asked somewhat quizzically, "Here? Ain't nuthin' here."

The quiet stranger tugged at Eddie's arm and the two men stood up, but the stranger did not answer the driver. He only tipped his hat and smiled as the driver shrugged his shoulders and pulled the lever to open the door.

The driver told them as they passed by his driver's seat, "Okay, then. Have a good day at work."

Eddie was thrilled, and he told the driver, "You too. See you on the flip-flop, driver!"

All that Eddie Bagley wanted to do was to go to work one last time.

He needed to complete the circle of life.

The two men stepped off the bus and onto the sidewalk as the bus pulled away in an envelope of smoke and fumes. The quiet stranger in the black hat did not say a single word, but he waved his hand to indicate for Eddie to follow him as they walked up the sidewalk, towards rows of industrial buildings which lined up along the roadway.

The two men walked up to a dark and somewhat foreboding door on a large warehouse type building, and Eddie commented as the quiet stranger slipped a key into a lock, "Fancy boots too. Make a nice clicking noise when you walk. We must be the first ones in the shop today. I might have to fire guys today if they keep coming in so late. Hate to do that to guys who have families to support, but you have to be committed and get here on time. We have production schedules to keep."

The quiet stranger did not say a word. He carefully slid the door open and the two men stepped in, as the quiet stranger in the black hat flipped on a light switch, and pulled the door closed behind them. The lights flickered to life and illuminated an amazing setting of a pristine and immaculate machine shop. Lathes, milling machines, grinders, polishers, tool cabinets, a caged tool crib and hand tools on workbenches, all carefully lined up in a perfect row upon perfect row. All the machines had oil mats carefully set in front of each machine and a clean, highly polished painted floor shone brightly in the newly lit lights.

Mr. Eddie Bagley stood there in the doorway . . . he was in awe. The old machinist's eyes were continually scanning the fantastic scene in front of his eyes. Tears appeared in his eyes and rolled down his cheeks. His mouth quivered and his hands shook.

Sometimes, in this life, in order to purge the pain and preserve our souls, our tears need to fall like rain.

Eddie reached up and he gently wiped the tears from his eyes. It was as if he did not want to lose this moment or the tears. This was his dream; this was his wish, to go to work one last time.

To turn one more part on a turret lathe.

After a few minutes, Eddie regained his purpose and his mission.

"Okay, sorry about that. It is now time to go to work, big man," Eddie said as he turned and looked at the quiet stranger who waved and led Eddie through the many rows of machines, until he stopped in front of one lathe. He pointed first at Eddie and then to the machine.

Eddie studied the lathe and smiled as he said, "You

know, for a fancy-dressed chip sweeper, you sure know your machines. I might promote you soon if you keep up the good work. Twelve-inch swing. Turret lathe, don't need them fancy-ass CNC puppies. This will do it! Sure, does feel good to be here. I am tired of hearing all that bullshit about the circle of life."

The quiet stranger in the black hat nodded, smiled and reached down in a box next to the lathe and pulled out a piece of round stainless-steel stock. He handed it to Eddie, who studied it and ran his hand over it as he felt it in his hands and in his mind.

"Perfect, stock . . . about four inches and one quarter," Eddie mumbled, as he reached for the chuck key and loaded the metal into the chuck.

"Now, I set the dogs on the rail and swing this tool rest over. Don't need no damn blueprint, because I got it all in my mind. Let me see, what kinda cutter you boys have loaded here? Good, this tool will do for a rough cut. Gonna need a finish tool, my safety glasses and where are my calipers? Maybe, you can line that up for me there, fancy guy in the black hat. Go over to the tool crib and ask the attendant to sign us out a good tool and find my damn calipers. Bagley is the name. Tell him, I don't jam 'em, break 'em or scrap 'em. I am the boss here, ya know."

The quiet stranger nodded and went off in the direction of the tool crib as Eddie shouted to him, "Cuttin' oil. Get me some cuttin' oil and an oil rag and chip brush too!"

There in the relative quiet of the rows upon rows of inert machines, one lathe spun to life. In the hands of a master, it came to life, and a man who yesterday could not operate a television remote control or a door handle to his own pickup truck, went to work. An unsung hero of this world, who for forty-seven years, went to work every day, supported his family, and produced, now had one last gasp at the restoration of his dignity.

The human mind is the most amazing machine of all

machines, and most of it remains a mystery to the greatest scientists, doctors and thinkers of this world and beyond. Perhaps it always will and we are better off if it does.

It might just be that it is God's design.

In an hour or two, while Mr. Eddie Bagley whistled a happy tune, he created a perfect hitch for his pickup truck.

Out of stainless steel too, so it will not rust.

Eddie reached down and shut the machine off. While taking off his safety glasses, Eddie spun the chuck around, found the unlock hole and slipped the chuck key into the slot. After unlocking the chuck, he pulled the part out of the chuck and held it in his hands. The master machinist smiled as he ran his hands over the gleaming metal, and he held it in his hands as he measured the perfection with his calipers.

"Here you go there, big guy with the fancy hat and boots. Grind it a touch, polish it up and it is good to go. Better, grab your broom and sweep them chips up too. That is lost profit, ya know. Put all the chips in the chip box, and when it is full, we will call the fork truck to take it to the loading dock. I will sit over here by the door. Old Eddie is a little tired, and we missed our coffee break time. In fact, I think it is almost quittin' time now."

The quiet stranger in the black hat smiled, and he finally spoke as he held the hitch in his hand, "Nice work, Eddie. Yes, you are correct, Eddie. We are done now. It is almost time to go home."

After a few minutes, the quiet stranger in the black hat met Eddie by the door to the machine shop. Eddie stood up from a chair he was sitting upon as the quiet stranger met him and put his arm around the old machinist.

The quiet stranger spoke, "Say, Eddie, I need one of these for my truck. Do you mind if I take this one and we will make another one some other day?"

"Sure, no trouble! You need it more than I do. We will make some more tomorrow! On a chip sweeper's pay, you cannot afford too much. Work hard and someday, you will run this shop!"

The quiet stranger in the black hat smiled, and he gently led Eddie out of the shop. He shut the lights off, closed, and locked the door. The sun was now up and the day was starting, and the streets were busy with traffic. They stood on the sidewalk in the bright sunlight as the quiet stranger in the black hat studied the traffic passing by in front of them. Eddie was still in a state of euphoria, and whatever fog had cleared when he was reliving his past glory had now returned. He stood next to the quiet stranger in the black hat while deeply immersed in a haze.

When the quiet stranger spotted a police car on patrol, he gently led Eddie by his arm over to the street while waving down the police car. The police car quickly pulled over and stopped next to the curb.

The quiet stranger in the black hat leaned in and explained to the officer who had rolled down the window, "This is a man who I am sure that his family is frantically searching for. He is very lost and confused. You might want to check with your dispatch and contact them right away to let them know that he is unharmed. His name is Eddie Bagley. Five Cliffwood Court in Franklinville, New Jersey."

The police officer nodded and grabbed his pen and a pad as he jotted down the information. Without further instructions, the quiet stranger in the black hat led Eddie to the rear of the patrol car; he opened the door and motioned for Eddie to step in. Initially, the police officers did not question the quiet stranger. Silently and ominously, the stranger commanded respect wherever he went.

"Say, thank you there, chip sweeper," Eddie said while reaching out to shake the stranger's hand. "Will I see you tomorrow for work?"

The quiet stranger in the black hat gently shook Eddie's hand and then he stepped back, tipped his hat, and nodded while saying, "Rest now, Eddie. This car will bring you home. As far as work goes, yes, you will see me tomorrow, Eddie. For work and a lot more."

Eddie smiled widely and proudly and said, "Good, we will make another hitch. Out of stainless, so it doesn't rust."

The police officers jumped out of the patrol car as the quiet stranger made sure that Eddie was in the rear seat and he closed the door.

One of the officers asked, "Geez, pal. Can you listen for instructions first or what? We *are* the police, ya know, just in case you didn't notice that fact. Can you give us a little more on the old guy here? Where did you find him?"

The quiet stranger in the black hat did not answer them.

When the quiet stranger did not answer them, one of the police officers abruptly asked, "Just who the hell do ya think ya are? Let's see your identification!"

Still, there was no answer or reaction from the quiet stranger in the black hat; instead, he stared intently at them with his dark, piercing, black eyes. The two police officers felt an ominous presence from the quiet stranger; one of them even nervously fingered the holster of his gun.

However, they did not pursue the questioning or react; the stranger's presence would not allow them to move. It was as if they were both helpless. The two officers froze in both time and reactions and they both felt as if the air all around them had suddenly turned intensely cold. It was a deep freeze, which caused the two officers to shiver in the briskness. After what seemed to be more than just a few short seconds, the standoff ended. The quiet stranger in the black hat smiled. He then tipped his hat, turned and walked briskly away. The police officers stood there and watched until he disappeared from their view and they no longer heard the click of the metal tips of his boots on the sidewalk.

Later that same evening, Mr. Eddie Bagley, at the ripe old age of eighty-eight, passed away peacefully in his sleep, in his own bed, in that fancy house in the senior living neighborhood.

The neighborhood where all the mailboxes were identical.

Eddie Bagley passed from this world in glory, because before he passed, he regained his dignity.

Mrs. Bagley, of course, was terribly upset. She felt as if her error had caused Eddie's condition to weaken, but the doctors explained that was not the case that it was just time and part of the circle of life. That tricky heart valve finally gave out and would no longer work. Everyone also pointed out how Eddie was in such wonderful spirits when the police officers returned him home. He went on and on about how a chip sweeper, who dressed in a fancy hat and boots that made a clicking noise when he walked, went to work with him and he had helped him make a hitch for his pickup truck.

It was also easy to see that Eddie died with the most remarkable smile on his face, and he held in his hands a piece of turned stainless steel that he made in the trade school many years ago. Eddie saved it and kept it in a drawer next to their bed.

There was a beautiful funeral service for Eddie Bagley. Family, friends, and the upper management from the machine shop all attended. It was very touching and before they closed his casket, Mrs. Bagley placed that special piece of turned stainless steel in her husband's hands. She had to do it. The piece was so special, and it was one of the first things which he ever created.

The graveside service was short, there was not too much else left to say. When you are speaking about a quality man such as Mr. Eddie Bagley was, there was nothing left to talk about any more.

Mrs. Bagley and her children and grandchildren, as well as a few close friends, lingered at the gravesite for a long time. As they were standing in a group, Mrs. Bagley noticed a very tall, lean, yet powerfully built man, standing next to a tree a few graves away.

The man standing next to the tree was dressed all in black; he wore a black vest covering a perfectly pressed black buttoned-up shirt, and his sharply creased black trousers had no ripples or wrinkles. On his head, he wore a wide-brimmed black hat.

There, from a distance, watching the graveside service conclude, was the quiet stranger in the black hat.

Mrs. Bagley first recalled the police officer's testimony when they brought Eddie home, when they told her that a very large man dressed in a black hat and black boots found her husband. They told her that the man was a bit unusual, and before he walked away, the stranger had provided them with very vague details about how he found Eddie. She also recalled Eddie happily speaking endlessly after he returned from his adventure, telling her about a chip sweeper, dressed in a fancy hat and fancy boots that made a clicking noise when he walked. The man dressed all in black took him to work, to a marvelous machine shop, a perfect shop. The best shop that he had ever seen. There, in the perfect shop, they made a new hitch for his truck.

This was all so very strange.

Mrs. Bagley excused herself from the conversation, and the group watched as she slowly walked away and moved towards the tree where the quiet stranger in the black hat stood.

Her son pursued her, concerned that she was going to speak with a stranger, but Mrs. Bagley stopped him and told him, "No, please. I will be fine. It is going to be fine, but I do need to speak in private with this man . . . he is a friend. I can tell."

Her son nodded, stood, and watched, as did the rest of the group.

It was very puzzling.

Mrs. Bagley approached the quiet stranger, and when she was close; he nodded, smiled and tipped his hat to her. She was amazed at his appearance. He was the largest man that she had ever seen, but she had no apprehension at all of being in his presence. There were no ominous feelings at all associated with the stranger.

"Somehow, and I cannot explain why, but deep inside of me, I felt as if Eddie was telling me the truth when he told us all about you. It was all so vivid to him. He was so happy when he returned. I thought that was so strange," Mrs. Bagley told the quiet stranger. She reached out her hands, and the quiet stranger took them and held them gently. She felt an incredible warmth emitting from his hands. It was very calming and reassuring.

"You are real, and not just a figment of his haziness and condition."

The quiet stranger smiled, nodded, but he still did not say a word. Mrs. Bagley looked deeply into his dark eyes and she swore that she could see a reflection of Eddie in them.

"I do not need to know who, or what you are, to know that you are here on a mission of hope, joy and of kindness. A mission, to help me understand that there is so much more to this life, and to this world, than what we all will ever really understand. Yet, it is wonderful to know that you are here, and that what you did for Eddie during his last day, meant so much to him that he felt it was time to leave this world and go off to another. Is that your reason for being here, quiet stranger? To reassure us all that there is so much more to life than just all of this."

Mrs. Bagley turned and waved her hands in the direction of the grave markers.

"Please, tell me that there is more to life than just this. Cold stark graves lined up all in rows. . .."

The quiet stranger in the black hat nodded. He let go of Mrs. Bagley's hands and reached inside of his vest pocket.

He pulled out the trailer hitch that Eddie made and held it in his hands. He nodded with his head to indicate for her to take it. She did so, and a rain of tears ran down her cheeks as she held the marvelous piece of steel in her hands.

Sometimes, in this life, in order to purge the pain and preserve our souls, our tears need to fall like rain.

She rubbed her hands over it and admired the glint and gleam of the steel in the glorious sunshine.

"It is marvelous. Remarkable." Mrs. Bagley said, as she marveled at her husband's skills and craftsmanship.

"Until he was stolen from me, he was so talented."

Those words struck a chord with the quiet stranger and he finally spoke, in a low, deep, melodious voice, "The best part is that he made it out of stainless steel and it will never rust."

He smiled as she smiled back when she recalled Eddie's words.

They grasped hands again and the quiet stranger said, "No, Mrs. Bagley, Eddie was not stolen from you. He is still with you forever, in the craftsmanship of that wonderful piece of metal, in the glorious sunshine of this day of his glory, in his heart and in your heart too. Eddie Bagley will never leave you because soul mates are forever."

Mrs. Bagley tried in vain to wipe the rain of tears from her eyes, while saying, "Thank you for restoring his dignity and for helping him complete the circle of life, quiet stranger. Is that what you do for us in this world?"

The quiet stranger nodded and softly said, "Yes, I do. Amongst a few other things, that is one of my missions. You see, the cruelness of this world can steal a person's mind, but it will never steal a person's soul. Until the very end, I guard the souls. I also try to restore the honor, to restore the pride, and to allow one, last, moment of joy, and glory before the ultimate glory arrives."

"Thank you for your mission. Dark stranger, did my dear Eddie tell you anything else?"

The Return of the Quiet Stranger in the Black Hat

The quiet stranger in the black hat gently let go of Mrs. Bagley's hands. He stepped back, looked over at Eddie's grave, then to the sky and he smiled widely. In the sunshine, she could study his handsome face, and she admired how his dark eyes sparkled with joy.

Finally, after adjusting his hat to hide his eyes and face, he told her, "Yes, he did. He told me that Bagley is his name. Tell them all that I don't jam 'em, break 'em or scrap 'em. I am the boss here, ya know."

The quiet stranger in the black hat smiled. He then tipped his hat, turned and walked briskly away. At first, he carefully and respectfully walked in and amongst the graves, walking gently upon the grass, between the flowers perched in brass vases on the graves.

He then picked up his pace and walked briskly towards the roadway.

The rest of her family and friends now joined Mrs. Bagley and together, the family stood and watched as the quiet stranger in the black hat reached the roadway of the graveyard.

Once he reached the roadway there, you could clearly hear the echo of the metal tips of his boots as they struck upon the asphalt surface of the roadway. Together, they all stood in the glorious sunshine and they bathed in the glory of the day. They stood and watched for a long time until he disappeared from their view and no longer could they hear the click of the metal tips of his boots on the roadway.

THE END

Epilogue

The old city's most notorious and elusive mobster, Mr. Tony Michanetti, and five of his henchmen, walked quickly across the main lobby of a downtown high-rise building. His henchmen, as well as Tony, never wanted to be "exposed" for too long in public. While they briskly walked through the lobby, one or two of the henchmen jumped up and pulled at the security cameras mounted on the walls, so that the cameras now all pointed down towards the floor. A security officer, sitting at a desk in the lobby, stood up, yelled at the group in protest, and then quickly sat down when he realized whom the culprits were.

Everyone in the old city knew who Tony was.

The group moved to the lobby elevators, and one of his men pushed the elevator button as the rest of the group surrounded Tony. With their eyes, they constantly scanned the lobby for any "intruders."

One of the elevators arrived at the lobby floor, the doors opened, and a young man dressed in a suit and tie looked out from inside the car.

"Out! Now!" The leader of the henchmen screamed and pointed, as the young man looked at the group, nervously nodded and he quickly scurried out of the elevator car.

The henchmen surrounded Tony and they quickly escorted him into the elevator. The lead man pushed the button for the tenth floor and the group relaxed as they watched the elevator doors slowly close. Just as the doors were slamming shut, a long and powerful arm suddenly appeared between the closing doors. The doors immediately lurched open, and the group stood there staring at a very large, tall, man dressed all in black, standing in the lobby, and staring back at them. His black vest covered a perfectly pressed black buttoned-up shirt, and he wore a wide-brimmed black hat upon his head.

He was the quiet stranger in the black hat.

"Sorry, pal, but this elevator car is full. Hit the road, asshole. Take the next one! BEAT IT!" The leader of Tony Michanetti's gang yelled as he waved at the door to indicate to the quiet stranger not to enter the car.

The quiet stranger only stared at them, and the entire group felt an ominous presence come over all of them. It seemed as the air temperature suddenly plummeted inside the elevator car because a cold chill filled the elevator car and the men found that they were all shivering in the cold air.

The quiet stranger ignored the instructions from the leader of the henchmen. The elevator doors cycled and once again started to close. The quiet stranger effortlessly pried the closing doors open with a quick movement of his arms. He then stepped into the car. The elevator doors slowly closed behind him, and he shook his head to indicate that he was not leaving.

The leader recovered from the strange encounter and shouted, "Are you stupid or friggin' deaf? GET THE HELL OUT! CAN'T YOU SEE THERE ARE SIX OF US HERE AND THAT YOU ARE ALONE? WE WILL BEAT YA ASS RAW!"

When the quiet stranger in the black hat only stared at them and did not heed the warning, the leader of the henchmen now sensed the danger, and he looked to Tony for orders. Tony first looked nervously at the group, and then to the immense man standing right in front of him.

The quiet stranger stood there, staring. His dark eyes sending shock waves through all of them.

Tony waved his hand in a frantic order, and all of his henchmen reached into their suit jackets, when the quiet stranger in the black hat held his arms and hands up in the air, to indicate to them to stop.

He then spoke in a low, melodious voice, "And do you really think that six men will be enough? I have to ask you, do you really think that if you had six-thousand henchmen to help you, do you think that it would be enough? It will not be enough. I can assure you that it will not be enough. Do not even bother with pulling the triggers. None of your weapons will fire."

"SHOOT HIS ASS!" Tony screamed.

The henchmen all pulled their weapons at once and frantically squeezed all the triggers, only to find out that the quiet stranger was correct because none of their weapons would fire. The quiet stranger in the black hat smiled. He tipped his hat and nodded to the now cowering and terrified, Tony Michanetti and his defenseless henchmen.

The quiet stranger said, "A close friend of mine, named, Charles McCracken, told me to tell you that he can't stand crooks, connivers, chiselers, and thieves. Unfortunately for you, Tony, as well as all of your henchmen here, I share my friend's sentiments."

He then reached over to the elevator buttons and pushed one button, while quietly saying, "Sorry, Tony, but today you are going down. Really, really, far, down."

ABOUT THE AUTHOR

If you ask Paul John Hausleben, he will tell you that he is not an author, he is just a storyteller. His mission is to continue to write and tell stories to warm your heart, make you laugh, and sometimes make you cry, just a little. Most of all, he deals in memories, and helps you to remember the good times of your own life, and the special people who touched you along the way. Paul was born and raised in Paterson, and then nearby Haledon, New Jersey, and began writing at an early age. He revisited a writing career later in his life, and he now is the author of a number of novels, compilations, short stories and audio and video works. Most of his work touches upon nostalgic remembrances of simpler times, and tells the stories of heartfelt, humorous, and special human relationships. Other than writing, among many careers both paid and unpaid, he is a former semi-professional hockey goaltender, a music fan and music reviewer, an avid sports fan, photographer and amateur radio operator. He now resides in Somewhere, U.S.A., but his heart always remains along Belmont Avenue in good old Paterson, and Haledon, New Jersey.

Other short story collections by Mr. Hausleben that you also will enjoy:

The Autumn Collection

Tales of the Quiet Stranger in the Black Hat

Casa Al Mare
A Jimmy Reeves Adventure
Featuring the Quiet Stranger in the Black Hat

The Christmas Tree and Other Christmas Stories.
Tales for a Christmas Evening

The Summer Collection

The Spring Collection

The Pool in Bethesda
Adventures of the Quiet Stranger in the Black Hat

Reflections. The Christmas Collection

And a few others too

Coming soon?

Published by God Bless the Keg Publishing
Somewhere, U.S.A.
You may write to the publisher at
Godblessthekegpublishing@gmail.com

"Life's simple pleasures are so often the best ones!"

Paul John Hausleben

www.ingramcontent.com/pod-product-compliance
Lightning Source LLC
LaVergne TN
LVHW010659110826
845149LV00014B/3168
9780990697961